Return of the Goatman

Return of the Goatman

Lawrence Weill

Seventh Star Press

Cover design: Olivia Pro Design

Cover art in this book copyright © 2024 Olivia Pro Design and Seventh Star Press, LLC.

Editor: Stephen Zimmer

Published by Seventh Star Press, LLC.

ISBN Number: 979-8-9861185-4-3

Seventh Star Press

www.seventhstarpress.com

info@seventhstarpress.com

Publisher's Note:

Return of the Goatman is a work of fiction. All names, characters, and places are the product of the author's imagination, used in fictitious manner. Any resemblances to actual persons, places, locales, events, etc. are purely coincidental.

Printed in the United States of America

First Edition

For Susan

Chapter 1

His long gait took the man quickly through dense woods. Tufts of spring grasses pushed up among the edges of a creek bank and the faint gurgle and trickle of the stream swallowed what little sound he made.

He weasel-walked along a faint game path, rolling his feet from out to in as he stepped, making as little sound as possible while still trying to make good time. Leaning his lanky body forward, his sinewy arms swept the low pine and water willow branches aside, creating a soft whoosh, making small drops of water sprinkle his shaggy grey-black hair and beard with the holy water of the morning's dew as he passed. He walked inexorably downhill, following the path that wended through the forest, keeping the creek to his left, sometimes within view, but always within earshot.

He had swung his bag up onto his shoulders, making straps of thin ropes tied to the grommets and a pack out of the small tarp, folded over and over itself to make a primitive rucksack with two braided twine straps. He had winnowed down what he was carrying to lighten his load, but there were still things he needed, living off the land amidst the trees, as well as a few things he would not give up, even if they were superfluous.

He took familiar steps. He knew the woods. Not these woods in particular, at least not yet, but he knew everything there was to know about forests in general. He was proud of his knowledge of the woods, how it created for him a kind of mutual respect; him for the forest and, in its own way, the forest for him.

He loved how the forest worked, and that was how he saw it. It worked. The forest lived as an organism unto itself. It breathed through the leaves and breezes that sent tiny insects and fertile motes flittering into the budding canopy and below to the bosky floor. Other insects devoured these offerings, ate leaves and twigs of the woodland behemoths, breaking all of it down into new loam.

Birds gathered moss and grasses and wove them into perfectly shaped nests, sheltered by branches. They ate berries and seeds of the trees and bushes, spreading them from the competition of their mother plants. Small rodents burrowed underneath to hide from predators, loosening the soil, so air and water reached the roots of the great trees. Fungi sprung forth, breaking down the dead matter on the forest floor and on fallen trunks. Larger animals kept the population in check so that a delicate balance was maintained.

Rivulets and rain showers provided the lifeblood of this creature-of-many-creatures, bringing essential water to everything within. To the man, it was at once a robust, hardy beast, and yet a delicate one that too often was pulled out of balance by chance natural occurrences, such as floods and fires, but more often by his fellow humans, who saw only land to build subdivisions on, or trees to be turned into lumber, or some other resource to be used up and forgotten. And while floods and fires also played a sometimes-beneficial role as a kind of meta-force of nature, when people were the cause of the change, it was almost always permanent and negative.

So this trek he made now was, as it always was, a kind of pilgrimage, a sacred walk through holy ground. It was all the more solemn when he let his mind wander to his destination, for at long last, he actually had a destination other than simply moving among the constituent parts of this forest beast simply to be conjoined within. If he was always at home in the forest, now he was headed to another home: the clapboard house he had once lived in at the edge of a small village. That small hamlet, downstream now from where he sojourned, straddled the confluence of two small rivers, which then merged into the somewhat larger Flint River, which flowed down the valley towards the city, where it combined again with yet another stream. Then it gushed past vast fields of soybeans and corn, around weirs and silty islands, fed by ever more rivers and creeks, past towns and cities teaming with cars and smoke, until it finally flowed into the Mississippi River. Then, these very waters he listened to now, just out of his line of vision, sped south, into the delta and out into the gulf, waters set free from river currents, only to be caught up the great streams of the oceans. And the tiny creek he now used as a guide held the molecules of hydrogen and oxygen and forest essence that would ultimately crash upon some distant beach, eliciting squeals from children at play.

If a part of him was always aware of this balance, this circularity, he ignored it now. His steps were deliberate, if still stealthy. His mind took him back to this house he was headed for, his once-home, the one he had one day simply walked away from, without forethought or plan, without anger or recrimination, except to himself. He didn't dislike the house he lived in before. Rather, he took a certain pride in how naturally it sat at the edge of the meadow, out the end of the road near town. He liked its compact neatness, its efficient use of space, its layout not remarkable, but well suited to him and his son.

His son. The recollection was always sobering. He had mourned his son in the only way he knew, by living the life he had taught Bobby to live, natural, resourceful, taking only what was absolutely needed and using every last piece of everything, in as many ways as possible. He had taught the boy about camping in primitive shelters, making fires from whatever was available, fishing and hunting with an expertise few could rival. He had helped him learn what seeds he could eat and what grasses to gather to nibble, or to soften a bed, or to weave into a sieve, if need be. They had hammered the sinew from a deer into threads and sewn together garments of tanned elk hide using a needle they had fashioned by splitting and re-splitting the leg bone of a deer carcass they came across, then sharpening and shaping it on sandstone. He had taught him everything he held dear.

If the boy's mother had shown no interest in helping raise their son, leaving one day on a "vacation," as she called it, and never returning nor even writing to inquire about either the man or the boy, he himself had taken it upon himself to share everything with his son. The two of them had bonded in a depth the man never knew he himself could plumb. And then, Bobby too was gone. It was a mission, they had told him, that the boy, a man and a soldier now, had volunteered for.

And he had come back to the man in a casket with a flag on it.

But the truth was, the man had also avoided mourning. If his going off to live as a kind of woodland hermit was an homage to the life of his son, it was also avoidance of the many reminders of his son in their home. The woven pieces of driftwood, made to look like an eagle taking off, that stood on the sagging porch reminded him too much of his son, taken far too soon in some distant land that even now the man found almost too foreign to be pronounced. Bobby had made the primitive sculpture when he was very young, maybe ten, and had presented it to his father as a birthday present. He had no money for a present, and no mother to take him to town even if he had had money, so he had spent weeks gathering the scraggly sticks and wedging them together. It was a far better gift than anything that might have been purchased anywhere.

So many memories.

The drawings Bobby made, first as a child, primitive and awkward pictures of the two of them camping or fishing, then later, of fish and deer and foxes and whatever else was around, so carefully drawn, intricately shadowed. The recurve bow they had made in the workshop from a black locust tree near the house was leaning up in the bedroom corner, just where Bobby left it when he went off to the service. The man never dared move it.

He wondered now if the bow or anything else was left in the house. Was the house even there still? It had been a long time. How many turns of the seasons had it been? Three? Four? No, more. He couldn't recall just now, but several years, at the least. Maybe the place had fallen apart. Or kids burned it, bored and mischievous and destructive. The house was isolated enough that any manner of things might have happened. Who would know? Maybe his sister, Susan, if she still bothered to check on the place. Why should she? If he didn't care what happened to it, why should she?

The man stepped into a puddle made by a slight oxbow in the stream and hidden by a clump of bushy beard leaning over the small pool. The icy spring water soaked immediately into his shoes through to his toes. The chill and dampness brought him out of his thoughts and back into his immediate surroundings. Most times, he would simply march on. But he did worry about the soaked socks losing their cushion and thereby causing a blister, and for once, he actually had another pair of socks. In fact, he had new socks, given to him by his friend who lived far up the hillside, many miles away now, but still there within his thoughts.

The man sat on a horizontal tree trunk, a remnant of one of the forest's great pillars, felled by age and weather. He changed into the new socks. They felt wonderful. New socks were such a simple pleasure, and he enjoyed the feeling. Yes, the wet shoe would no doubt make the sock within damp again, but it would dry.

He looked around him before standing. Shagbark hickories, red oaks, white oaks, yellow poplars surrounded him, guarded him. There was a hawthorn, the bark of its twisted trunk no doubt full of bugs. A few white pines grew nearer the stream. An eastern wood pewee flitted from a crevice in a boulder, caught a lemon skipper fluttering by, hovered for a moment, then returned to his hiding spot. The man smiled. The woods were alive and healthy.

Standing, he resumed his journey. It was coming on midday and his stomach reminded him to eat something. He swung his pack around as he walked and grabbed a strip of dried rabbit from just under the flap, and gnawed on the leathery meat. He needed more, but there would be time later for that.

He made a point of looking in the shallow pools of the creek next to him as he walked. A few had tiny fish in them. He would seine for some fish for dinner. They were very small, and he could simply fry them whole in what he had left of the venison tallow he had rendered several days before. That would be a good use for it. He needed to use it up, and it wouldn't take all that long to get home.

He had wandered across the country, over the years, but when he had decided to go back, he had been already closer than he had been in a long time. Perhaps it was his encounter with the old man grieving atop the hill that convinced him to go home. Or perhaps he was already heading there when he met him, and that was why he was as close to Wyler's Ford as he had found himself. So close to home.

He gave himself a soft snort for thinking it. Home. He was home right where he was. But that was different. People didn't get that. Most people went to the woods to get away; he went to get back. He knew his mindset was different from most people's. He recalled now being confronted in a park one morning when he crawled out of his leaf hut. The park ranger stood there in his brown and green uniform, his green campaign hat sitting too high on his head, strapped to his chin. His hands crossed behind him, he stood as if in military formation, at ease.

"Excuse me, sir?" the ranger had asked blandly, as if he was accustomed to seeing tall, gaunt, grubby, naked men crawl out of piles of leaves deep in the underbrush. The man had been so taken aback by this intrusion, he had only stood there for a moment, making sense of it all, before looking down at himself and stepping behind the branches of a small maple for whatever cover the leaves might provide. The ranger had not responded with rancor or anger, only matter-of-factly said, "That's quite a shelter you have there."

"Thank you," he had croaked in response, his voice box unaccustomed to speaking much.

"That notwithstanding, it isn't permitted for homeless people to camp out in the park." The ranger didn't scowl, but neither did he smile.

"I'm not homeless," he recalled saying more plainly as he squatted down behind a boulder.

"I beg your pardon?" The brim of his hat raised only slightly.

"I have a home." He waved towards the hut.

"Sir, a pile of leaves is not a home."

"But it is. To me, anyway."

"Well, it's not a proper house."

"So people in tents have a proper house?"

"Sir, that's not what I mean."

"What do you mean?" he remembered asking, wishing he could crawl back into the shelter and dress, or, at the least, relieve himself, which was why he had climbed out in the first place.

"You know what I mean, sir. People who live in piles of leaves obviously don't have homes." He had sounded more peeved.

The man had stood now, no longer worried about his exposure. "How is that obvious? I don't get that."

The ranger had brought forth a free hand and waved dismissively at him. "I don't have time to debate the point. Please get yourself dressed, take down this brush pile, which is a fire hazard anyway, and move along." The park ranger now raised his chin, as if that made the discussion complete. The brim of his hat rose like a faint horizon.

"Okay. Okay," he had muttered, shaking his head, and climbed back into his hut. "'You beat everything, you know that, Barn?'" he mumbled.

"What was that?" the ranger had called from outside.

"Nothing. Nothing." And he had moved on, just as he had been ordered to. He had been scores of places since then and learned to avoid being seen so as not to be banished. Preemptive banishment was better than prescribed banishment, the way he saw it. At least he was escaping the judgmental frowns and shaking, accusatory heads.

Was that the turning point? Was that encounter with the officious ranger when he had begun living like an escaped convict, hiding from people, dodging populated areas? He had managed to stay out of sight, for the most part.

There were a few he had met, but it rarely turned out well. There were farmers who were certain he would pillage the gardens and so threatened him from a distance, pointing small caliber rifles at him as if he were a rodent filching carrots. There were county deputies, slowing their cruisers to eye him warily as he disappeared into the forest, looking like a thin, bearded yeti. And there were the dogs. They were more serious challenges, their sense of smell being so acute they followed him for miles, sometimes playfully, sometimes menacingly, until he would backtrack along the trail and then into a stream, leaving the hounds lost and confused. Then there were the very few people he had had good interactions with. A few downtrodden, the woman who had traveled with him for a bit, the old man he had become friends with on a forgotten farm atop the hillside. But mostly, he hid.

But he wasn't a criminal. He broke no laws, as he saw it, except maybe the occasional trespass. But he was a better steward of the land than practically any of those who owned the land, as if wild woodlands could be owned by any man. Perhaps he was not so much a criminal as an outlaw. No, he obeyed the laws of nature. An outcast? Maybe. But no one had cast him out. He had journeyed out in a kind of holy quest, like some sort of lone crusader, a journeyman whose only destination was the journey itself. Neither outlaw nor outcast, he was more simply an outlier, he thought. And now, he realized, he had mistaken his journey for a holy quest when it was merely a windmill; and he was no more than a modern-day Don Quixote.

Now he felt the ground rising with each step, a berm

beneath his boots that told him he was nearing where this small brook he followed dropped into a larger stream. What would Bobby think if he saw him now? Bobby would have loved him. He would have smiled at his father and walked with him, and together, they would have gone home. The man stood now on the bank of the creek with its tangles of limbs and debris from a past flood. He turned and followed the stream, downstream, to where it would return him to their home.

Chapter 2

He followed the creek down through a narrow, heavily wooded valley, across an open field, and back into the deep thickets. He made camp that night, as he often did, by simply unrolling the tarp and putting half of it under his bedroll and the other half over him to keep the dew off in the morning. He didn't want to spend the time setting up and tearing down. This was only a stop along the way, not a camp.

He pulled out his casting net he had tied together from sections of the ball of string his friend had given him, a painstaking task of tying tiny but tight knots at very regular, short intervals. He had made weights for it using small stones he wrapped in bits of wire he found along abandoned backroads. It was primitive-looking and not as large as he might have liked, but it worked.

Twisting his torso, he swung the net with a smooth, fluid motion out into the slow-moving water and let the weights sink. Then he pulled in the long lead line. He quickly had several very small shad, and one somewhat larger pumpkinseed that was big enough to clean. That was all he needed for tonight. It had been successful enough that he could use it in the morning, he decided, if he didn't mind carrying a damp net along as he went through the woods.

He cleaned and scaled the sunfish and, together with the small shad cooked whole, he fried them all up with some wild ramp greens he found along the way. The fish and greens spattered and sputtered in the battered aluminum pan he had carried for more years than he could recall. He had found it tossed away in a trash bin near a state park. It was scratched and dented and stained when he found it, so it was easy to see why someone had thrown it away, but it was functional. He had boiled drinking water almost daily, since most streams he found he distrusted. There were often livestock somewhere upstream and runoff from fields treated with chemicals, so the extra step made him feel much safer. The fish was satisfying and filling. He ate a few leaves of wood sorrel to fill out the meal, but the truth was, he had never really acquired a taste for it. It was terribly sour.

The next morning, he braced himself with a tea made from pine needles and headed downhill again. It wasn't easy going. Scrubby bushes often crowded over the path, making finding his way all the more difficult. In places, rusty barbed-wire fences either stretched down into the stream, or, more often, spiraled loosely around some narrow post, long since rotted away at the bottom. The loose wire was more hazardous to navigate than the taut wire, and being scratched with rusty barbed wire was definitely not on his list of things to try.

In other places, smaller feeder steams crossed his path, sometimes leaving deep, steep creek beds to try to climb down, across, and over. Sometimes, he walked back up the new creek until he found a place to cross. Other times, he simply waded across, his faded, stained, now-grey pants dripping with muddy water as he climbed out the other side.

The stream now was more river than creek, and that too made the trek different. Every now and then, there were a few more roads, dirt roads leading through a spent timbering zone, or lanes along the edge of a furrowed field with twin paths of crushed limestone for a farmer's tractor to pass through the mud, and even a few paved roads that led to riverside houses and retreats. This last part was new for him.

He generally avoided populated areas, but now, he strode

down narrow, blacktop roads, thankful for the easier walk, but wary of anyone who might feel threatened by a lanky, straggled-haired, shaggy-bearded stranger marching along the road looking like a scarecrow come to life without any Dorothy to soften the image. He made quick camps along the river, now grown wide enough for the occasional pleasure boat traffic or fishermen and women. The latter two, if they paid any attention to him at all, only nodded a slight tilt of their heads in acknowledgement of having seen him and went about their fishing.

He had walked on this route for a long time, knowing the way, when he began to see a few familiar landmarks that told him he was nearing what was, at long last, a destination. It was that liminal transition from the deep woods to more frequented forest. There were now paths through the woods.

Occasionally, there were tags of brightly colored tape tied around a tree trunk or along a fence row marking where a hunter had marked a route to his blind the previous season, but never thought to take down the tape. He even knew who owned this land, or at least, who used to own it, back when he had come here with Bobby to practice with his slingshot. As he strode through the woods, he recalled the meadow not far away, where at this time of year asters and bluebells were blooming.

Now he recognized where he was by a high-tension line crossing the river from the dam just below the village, taking the hydroelectric power off to the grid. Out in the current there was the muddy island in the middle of the Flint River where he had swum with his boyhood friends back in his youth, the few straggly trees jutting from its flat soil, still clinging to life despite floods and droughts.

Then he came across the railroad tracks that ran from the grain elevators at the edge of town and out across the green valley towards the city. So very often he had listened to the far-off horn of the train, lying in his bed at night. When he was young, it was a siren call to leave for bigger places, places that surely were more exciting, or at least less predictable than Wyler's Ford. But that predictability that was so anathema to him as a child was a kind of quilt when he grew older, a comforter, soothing, warm, calm. Then the train whistle at night no longer called him to leave, but merely reassured him, with the distinctive, if haunting, sound of home. He climbed the gravel railroad bed and followed the tracks towards town.

While he moved closer and closer to the town he knew so well, he thought about what he meant to do. What did he intend to do in Wyler's Ford? Maybe he would move back into the house, if it was still there, if it was even vaguely livable. He supposed if he could sleep in lean-to's made from rough-cut poles and a tarp, no matter what condition the house was in, he could make it work.

He had certainly stayed in as rough a camp as he could ever imagine. How bad could it be? He could fix it up again, if he wanted to. Did he want to? He had been a carpenter, after all. Still was, truth be told. Was it even possible for him to not be a carpenter? Once a carpenter, always a carpenter, the way he saw it. And he was pretty good at it, he would admit. He was certainly good enough to make a good living, even in a town as small as his.

Yes, he would fix the house all up. He would make it back into the home he and Bobby had filled with their lives. They had had so many good times there. They had told stories on the porch while he taught the boy to whittle. They had laughed at Bobby's bad jokes, laughing as much at how bad they were as anything. Even Nikki had loved to sit under the sassafras tree with them, wailing out 60's folksongs while he played the guitar and Bobby honked away badly on a tinny harmonica. Of course, that was before Nikki left.

Nikki.

He let himself wander there in his thoughts as he crossed a railroad trestle over the smaller of the two rivers that merged to form the broad, flinty shallows that had first been the reason for the start of the tiny hamlet. She had been everything he was not: adventurous, impulsive, flashy, daredevil. And she was pretty. Very pretty. How many times had he looked at her and couldn't believe his girlfriend was Nikki Salyers? He stared at her across the table at Cibo's Pizza, where they gathered after class in high school, or caught a sidelong glance at her next to him in the old truck he bought when he was seventeen, her long legs folded up to rest her bare feet on the dash. They spent every weekend cruising up and down Main Street, a four-block stretch that held the post office, the bank, the city hall, and the few stores that somehow remained in business despite the mall in Ashland pulling everyone to shop from fifty miles away.

He reached the opposite shore and made his way down the embankment of the tracks, using his arms to balance as his feet rolled beneath him on the gravel, half-walking, half-skating down the incline. He let himself return to the thought of how he and Nikki drove up and down the street on Saturday nights, stopping to talk to the other couples from their tiny school, sometimes drinking beer bought from the local bootlegger. Nikki always had a cigarette in her long, slender hand, with her long brown hair pulled into a ponytail through her Cincinnati Reds cap. How her dark eyes danced. And he saw the envy in his friends' faces and reveled in his good fortune.

He found now the dirt trails that crisscrossed along the riverbank where every kid in town had learned to fish by dangling bamboo poles over the slow-moving current, learned to swim by swinging out on the thick rope tied to the limb of a sycamore tree hanging out over the water, learned to love by sneaking off with each other to hardly discreet corners of the beaten-down grasses.

They were both heading off to school, he to Morehead, she to the big university, and they had vowed to keep true to each other despite the distance. They talked about it, between grappling in the cab of the truck on the lonesome gravel road they frequented and lying on the grass naked after skinny dipping in Barlow's Pond. They vowed their teenage love and how they would always be so in love. He would drive his rickety pickup every weekend to Lexington to see her, and they would write letters back and forth, every day.

But underneath the promises, both of them knew, high school was it, for them. He knew it the entire time he had told those lies to himself, saying them to Nikki, but trying to convince himself. They would go off to school, and it wouldn't take long. A girl as pretty as Nikki would be swarmed by guys at the university, and she was both brash enough and brave enough, she would go out with as many boys as she wanted to. And, truth be told, he wanted her to. Then.

They weren't really right for each other. His only claims to fame were, with his tall, angular body, he stood half a head taller than any other boy in school, and that he was a moderately good pitcher for their school team, the Lions. His was a local fame, a local prospect. Hers was an intellect, a personality, the charm, and the looks to take on the world. He knew he would come back to Wyler's Ford. She always talked about leaving and never looking back.

Then Bobby. They got pregnant and everything changed, he recalled, as he sidestepped a ring-necked snake sunning in the path. That sweltering July evening, when the chirrups of crickets were punctuated by the buzz of mosquitos, and the two of them had gone out for their usual escapades, Nikki was somber, preoccupied, and despite replying "Nothing" whenever he asked her what was wrong, he knew everything was turning. He just didn't know how much.

Now he found the trail that led to the de facto parking lot, no more than a rutted widening of the old dirt road. The path had always been surprisingly narrow for the expanses on each end, but in the early spring, the way was clear. It wasn't far now.

Nikki didn't smoke that night, didn't drink any of the tepid beer he had brought. She simply stared out the window, quietly, as he drove around, until finally he had driven up the Clark's ridge, the overlook above the river where already three darkened cars swayed rhythmically. He had parked the truck and turned to her. He remembered like it had happened last week.

"Nikki, what is it, honey?" He had tried to sound reassuring. He thought he knew what it was. She was probably dreading what she intended to do, which was to break up with him. He knew it. He thought he saw it coming. He steeled himself. "Is it someone else?" he finally managed.

She had spun to face him, her face shocked, angry, sad, uncomprehending. "No!" she yelled, then more softly, "Well, yes." She had turned and stared at the vinyl covering of the glovebox for a few seconds, then back at him. "But it's not what you think."

Then she had told him all of it, how she had missed a period and was starting to feel sickened by every little smell and how, eventually, her denial was overwhelmed by the evidence. Even now, walking back to his old hometown, as he reached the old road and turned toward the outskirts of town, he remembered the rush of feelings he had felt. His own confusion, surprise, anxiety, all mixed with an odd feeling of elation. The cab had grown quiet as they looked at each other, then out the windshield at the three-quarter moon, then back at each other. Then they had hugged, holding each other for a long time. Just hugging and crying.

The next few weeks remained a kind of blur, the wasted secretiveness, the anger on her father's face that never really went away, although he had been surprisingly doting on Bobby. There were tears and obvious attempts at bravery and supportiveness from his mother and Nikki's. His own father's reaction was the hardest one to read, a kind of resigned shaking of the head, his mouth a flat line of disapproval, but scarcely a word of reprobation or sympathy.

They had married and forsaken college, at least until they could "get it all together," as they often repeated to each other and to themselves. But they didn't get it all together, not in the sense they had meant it. He had gotten a job at the truss yard, nailing together the long boards for houses somewhere up the road they might never travel. They had moved into the cottage that had once been his grandfather's "pouting shack," as they called it, his retreat out on the edge of town. Nikki had cleaned it with her friends, a group of classmates who hovered around her with such sincere affection he had grown immediately aware of how much he liked his little hometown. And he himself had brought home scraps of wood from the yard to frame out cabinets and build a shed roof over the porch; and the little place became theirs, became them.

He reached the chip-and-seal road that led to town now. His sister's house was not far. A couple of miles, maybe. He remembered how he had settled in with his life with Nikki and then Bobby. If he had had to change his plans, still, he was happy. He did an apprenticeship with the carpenters' union, became a journeyman, and started building upscale cabinets for large houses being constructed overlooking the lake, fancy homes used only occasionally by wealthy families from Lexington, Cincinnati, and Louisville. But he wasn't jealous of them. It was a good income.

And for a while, Nikki also seemed happy, bustling around the house, taking care of Bobby, cleaning, sewing together curtains for the windows that were so old the glass was wavy from gravity. She cooked meals for them, barely edible ones at first, full of the errors of the neophyte cook, but eventually hearty and fulfilling, if never very fancy. It seemed like she was adapting and even growing into her new life. But when the holidays came, or summer breaks, and their friends returned from the colleges they had gone off to, he could see the wistful gaze on Nikki's face as they sat in the yard, pouring glasses of Boone's Farm and drinking Sterling beer around the campfire.

Their friends simply shared their new experiences, laughing at hijinks in the dorms or sorority houses. They talked about areas of study they never had any inkling of in high school, and now they were considering careers in advertising and social work. Even his own high school best friend, Jimmy, now spouted harebrained philosophical ideas that anyone could see were silly, but determined to press these ideas into the conversation.

"But you can't prove anything exists except yourself and your own consciousness," Jimmy had argued.

"Why would I want to?" was always his own reply.

Return of the Goatman

All of these ideas and adventures were simply their friends telling what they were doing, and never about reproaching anyone. But in doing so, they reminded Nikki of what might have been. He remembered seeing it in her far-away look, as their friends drove off down the dirt road from their little house, the light from the dying campfire glinting off the chrome of their bumpers, the red taillights brightening at the edge of the highway, then disappearing around the bend. He saw it in her posture the following days when friends visited, a kind of resignation both in her carriage and her behavior. Even their love-making, which tended to the passionate, became more subdued, tenderer, in its way, which he didn't really object to, but he understood the change.

He made the curve of the road and saw Susan's little bungalow. It looked the same. It could use a power washing, maybe, but still seemed solid. Her hydrangeas on either side of the front steps were greening up. The boxwoods were still neatly trimmed and lined up across the front, the bay window above them from the living room showing lacy curtains from inside. The wooden gate on one side was new, or maybe not new, but moved. Wasn't that gate at the back side of the yard before? He supposed she moved it.

As he made his way closer to the house, he wondered where the girls were, his nieces, Susan's bouncy, fair-headed girls who had loved to play "Flip the Monkey" with him, by holding his hands and climbing up his body step by step, to stand on his chest as he leaned back, then turning a back flip off him as he held onto their hands.

Susan came around the side of the house. Her hair was still blonde, and he wondered if that was her doing rather than Mother Nature. But she wasn't old, maybe mid-forties? He tried doing the math, but he really didn't know how long it had been. The seasons all blurred together. The years that had passed seemed like little more than heat waves off the pavement in the distance. Her hair was pulled in a ponytail. She wore faded jeans and a ragtag shirt, no doubt her yardwork outfit. She had on gloves too.

Susan wasn't looking his way. She dragged a hose around the edge of her bungalow, watering her flowers she always loved. He wondered what crop she was planting this year. She had always liked lilies and geraniums and especially loved her butterfly bushes. She looked the same. How was that possible?

He stopped in the road, some fifty yards from his sister, watching her. She was still slender, graceful, pretty. He had always been so proud of his little sister, "the prettiest girl in school," he had often told her, to her bashful but appreciative smile. Susan had been the most steadfast after Bobby died. She had spent long hours with him, puttering around his house to help clean, but really just being company to him. She had fixed him meals and made him eat, which was not easy, he recalled, his appetite drained by sorrow. He had grown up her protector as kids, but she had become his rock when he needed a foundation in a world suddenly bereft of mooring.

She tugged now on the heaviness of the water-filled hose, and being distracted from the watering, looked up. She saw him. But at first, she didn't see him, in particular, just some wayfaring old coot, maybe, wandering the backroads. Her gaze was as if she was looking far beyond him, at a cloud on the horizon behind him. Then her eyes opened wide with recognition, her jaw dropped, she let out a yelp, let loose of the hose, and ran towards him.

Chapter 3

His little sister sprinted towards him. He slipped the bag off his back and let it slide down his arms and onto the ground. Susan was crying as she ran. He took a step forward, but she was there already, a few steps away. She had covered the ground in a time athletes would have been proud of.

He braced himself and she threw herself at his chest. She wrapped her arms around his back, and he started to reach around hers, but she pulled back, took a step back, and looked up at him. Then she slapped him. Hard.

She looked like she wanted to slap him a second time, but then she hugged him again. Now he hugged her too, his face still smarting from the slap. But he understood. He had that much coming, at least. He had, after all, left without a word to anyone. It wasn't fair to Susan the way he had done it. It wasn't fair to anyone in his family. In his grief, he had been selfish, as if he were the only one in the world who mourned Bobby. He had been selfish and unthinking, and he had hurt the very people he cared the most about. Then Susan pulled back and looked at him.

"You stink, Robert," she said flatly.

"I know." He hung his head and looked at the ground. "I know. I shouldn't have left like that and . . ."

"No, you shouldn't have, but I mean you literally stink." Susan raised her eyebrows. "You smell like an old goat." Her look was stern. She was glad to see him, he knew, but she still had every right to weigh her anger at him for a bit. "Jesus, Robert, have you not bathed in the past six years?"

He raised his eyes to look at her. "Six…?"

"Where the hell . . .?" Susan started, then turning she said, "Wait, I got to turn off the water." She started trotting back towards the house. Robert was unsure whether he should wait, as instructed, or not. Then she stopped, turned, and put her hands on her hips and yelled at him, "You coming or not, Robert?"

She looked exactly like he remembered his mother looking when he would dawdle as a child, and he suppressed a giggle at the recollection. He leaned over and picked up his bag, but just now, he was not sure there was anything in there he needed, now that he was back. Maybe the recorder he had made and taught himself to play. He still had two new pairs of socks, some string.

Then, he put the inventory-taking out of his head and strode after Susan. She was trotting back towards the house, but with his long strides, Robert was catching up quickly. When she picked up the hose, she looked at it, then at Robert who was nearly there, then back at the hose. She pursed her lips and turned towards him. She put one hand on her hip and held the hose end away from her, the stream weeping out onto the lawn.

"So," she looked at him evenly. "You back now?" She tilted her head slightly.

Robert blinked, just for a moment confused by the question. He was standing there, wasn't he? Then he understood. "Yeah," he managed. He felt like he was gabbing his brains out, although he had only said a few words. He so rarely spoke any more, not since the woman who had traveled with him out west had said goodbye and trudged off into the scruffy wheatgrass and pinons of the New Mexico mountains, tired of his moodiness and sullen disposition. She had understood his grief, but just couldn't bring it upon herself to keep trying to break through. "Yeah, Sis, I'm back." He realized in saying it, by saying it, he had decided.

"Good," she said, but her tone was businesslike. "Come on." She started marching towards the rear of the house, her usual "take charge" posture evident. He followed. She carried the hose with her, a slow, steady shower of water squirting out the nozzle. Once through the gate, she closed it and waved him towards a corner of the yard where the tall wooden fence sheltered a lilac bush ready to bloom. "Strip down," she commanded.

"What?" Robert scowled.

"You're not coming into the house like that. Would take me months to get the smell out. Go on. Take it all off. It's not like I'm not your sister." She was still holding the hose as she turned and walked over to the little detached garage.

Robert shrugged. He put his tarp-become-knapsack on the round metal patio table that he remembered from before, then started pulling off his shirt. Or what was left of his shirt. It was a found shirt, rejected even by the Salvation Army and tossed into a bin behind the retail store somewhere in Oklahoma, maybe, or Arkansas. He couldn't recall. But it was mere tatters now. Susan returned with a black trash bag. He started to put the shirt next to the rucksack. "No, put it in here." She held the bag out as far as she could, and he took it. "I swear to God, Robert, you positively reek."

"Thank you," he managed, trying to send her a maybe wry smile, but his facial muscles didn't quite seem up to it yet. She was being honest, he knew. She wasn't intending to hurt him.

He tugged at his boots, tired, heavily creased lumps of leather, flattened beyond all recognition. He placed them on the concrete slab patio. "No, those too." He looked up at her, then picked up the boots and tossed them in.

He finished undressing and then Susan twisted the nozzle and sent a cold blast of water onto his naked body. He might have been accustomed to cold water after all this time in the wild, but it still chilled him. He wasn't sure what his role was exactly in this baptism back into civilization. He turned to be sprayed all over. His sister was being quite methodical and was perhaps trying to get him clean by pulverizing the dirt from his naked body. Finally, she came closer and handed him the nozzle.

"Here, you take over. Be right back." She turned and marched up the back steps onto the porch then into the house. Robert continued rinsing himself, adjusting the spray so the stream was a tad less brutal. Susan came out with a bottle of shampoo and a large, screamingly white bath towel. "Use this," she thrust the bottle at him. "All over," she said after a moment, when he had squirted a healthy glob onto his head.

"Yes, Mother," Robert smirked. But Susan didn't laugh. She crossed her arms and stared at her nude, still-hairy brother, showering in her backyard.

"You missed her funeral," she said finally, then turned and walked back towards the house.

All the air left Robert's lungs. He stood for a moment, his arms at his side, the bottle of shampoo in one hand, the hose in the other, spraying water in a mist the sun refracted within, a hazy rainbow in the corner of his vision. There was a fierce knot in his throat.

His thoughts raced through his head incoherently. He suddenly remembered scenes from childhood, his mother doting, scolding, hugging him. He felt slightly dizzy. The water sprayed on his feet.

The backdoor screen banged. "Finish up, Goatman. Water's not free, you know." He looked up at her and saw her look had softened. She was carrying some clothes, jeans, maybe, a tee shirt, all neatly folded in a pile, a pair of flip-flops on top. It showed that she had wounded him, and she regretted it, he saw.

She set her mouth in a thin line. Robert finished rinsing off and began drying. The towel felt as plush and full and soft as if it came from the finest hotel. He took the clothes and dressed. They were at the same time too big and too small. The waist was far too large, but the cuffs of the jeans came up well over his ankles.

They had been Johnny's, no doubt. Why she still had them was anyone's guess. Johnny had left Susan and the two girls and had the audacity to end up with Francis Creel, of all people. Robert didn't care just now how the clothes fit. Even the loose jockey briefs felt okay. They were clean. Robert felt better, clean, but it was all a bit much, yet.

"Mom," he started, but he wasn't sure how to finish. He took the steps two at a time, but unhurriedly, up to the porch.

"Two years ago, next month." Susan was pulling out a battery-operated hair trimmer from a cloth bag. She twisted a cola chair that sat next to a small bistro table and pointed at it. "Sit." Her voice was calm, even.

Robert rubbed his beard. He pushed his fingers through his hair. The shampoo evidently had a conditioner in it and his fingers untangled knots that had been there far longer than he cared to admit. But some of his knots felt too set to untie. He looked at his sister, who stood impassively, looking intently at him, the clippers held at her shoulder like a fully loaded pistol she didn't want to aim at anyone. She was the same no-nonsense Susan she had always been. He had been her hero when they were younger; then she was his anchor when he needed one.

"I didn't know," he finally managed.

"Yeah, well, you forgot to leave a forwarding address, Robert." But her tone was softer now. All he could do was look at the floor of the porch, painted sky blue and swept clean. Susan always took care of her place.

He looked back at her. "Dad?" He felt his stomach tighten.

Susan lowered the clippers now and stood behind the chair, her thin arms at her side. "Daryl has Papa at his house." She paused, then added, "In Louisville?"

"I know where Daryl . . ." Robert started, then trailed off. Who was he to get defensive about anything? And what was he quite sure he still knew?

"Yeah, well, have a seat, Robert. That pile on top of your head is beyond control." Her gesture now towards the seat was more invitation than command. He sat and Susan put a spacer on the clippers and began making paths across his head. "Dad is okay. Just getting older." She allowed a tender note in her voice.

"Miss him around here though."

Robert didn't answer. So many decisions had been made, had had to be made, while he was gone. He had certainly let people down. And not just people: family. In places, the trimmer became caught in the nests of tangled hair, which hurt his scalp, but Susan simply worked her way through as best she could. Huge clumps of greying hair fell around him on the porch floor, thick and still damp enough to occasionally land with a soft "thunk."

After a while, she changed the spacer and did a second run on the sides of his head. She had always cut Johnny's hair, but now that Robert recalled, not so well. But it would be okay. An old man had told him once, the difference between a good haircut and bad haircut was three days. And it had to look better than the ragtag mop of hair he had shown up wearing.

After a while, Susan stopped, appraised her work, and made some final trims at spots she had missed. She stood in front of him, shook her head, as if to say, "Oh well," then handed Robert a hand mirror from the cloth bag the clippers had come from.

Robert looked at his reflection. He had not seen himself except in the wavy images of darkened store fronts in years. The haircut was not the first thing he noticed: the cheekbones were. He was painfully thin, his eyes looked sunken. Even with the beard, he looked gaunt. Had he really done this to himself? Yes. Of course he had. Had he punished himself enough? Yeah, he thought, maybe he had. Susan handed him the clippers. "Here, work on the beard, Stinky." She stepped away to retrieve the broom by the backdoor.

"Hey, I took a shower," he protested.

Susan turned and gave a nod. "You took the first shower, you mean. After you get that beard cut back, you're going in and taking another." She paused. "And shaving off the rest of that mess on your chin. You look like Merlin on acid." Robert broke into laughter, and Susan smiled. "Welcome home, Robert." She left and went inside.

"Thanks, Sis." He turned on the clippers and, using the

mirror as his guide, took off the straggly beard.

He heard pots and pans rattling, the refrigerator door open and close. His mouth watered. Food. Actual meals. Susan had always been a good cook. Not fancy, usually, but hearty and always plenty. Robert trimmed the beard off, first in one direction, then another, then yet another. The beard fell to the floor next to the mess of his hair from his haircut. When he was done, he looked in the mirror and appraised himself.

How had Susan even recognized him, he wondered. He looked like a poster urging folks to support refugees. The height, he guessed. Most people remembered his height. Was he a refugee? It's true, he felt displaced. Displaced by war, yes, the war that took Bobby. But he had not been forced to leave; he left of his own accord.

No, he was no refugee. Just a coward, too afraid of his own reality to face life on its own terms. He was embarrassed now, sitting on the curled metal chair surrounded by his shorn hair. How brave had the boy been, only for the father to run off, to desert his post.

Robert stood, his energy suddenly drained by self-loathing. He went inside. The wooden screen slammed behind him. Susan was pouring penne pasta noodles from a box into a large pot of boiling water. Steam rose from another pan redolent with broccoli. A jar of Alfredo sauce was sitting next to the stove. All those years, and he remembered her making this dish. It was a go-to for her. Filling, satisfying, and quick to pull together.

He stood next to the stove, watching her movements. He had missed watching his sister's movements, so familiar, so, what? So Susan.

She stirred the noodles and reduced the heat. She turned and looked at him, all stooped over and feeling very defeated. She just gazed at him a moment. Her eyes watered. "It's okay, Robert. You're home now." She let the wooden spoon rest on the edge of the pot and now she put her arms around his neck and pulled him down toward her. She held him, his chin resting on her shoulder, his back bent. "You're home now," she said over and over. "You're home now."

He reached his long arms around to her back and hugged her. He had not been hugged in so very long. Tears welled in his eyes, and he let them flow down his cheeks.

"Home," he said finally, pulling away.

"Yes, E.T., 'Home.'" She flashed that smile he had always told her was her best attribute. He stepped back and glanced down at himself.

"So now I'm E.T.?"

"Your choice." She gave a rueful smile, then turned and stirred the pasta. She grabbed the pan with the broccoli in it and carried it to the sink. "But you're still a bit ripe. Ready for shower number two?"

"Okay, 'Goatman' I guess it is." He shook his head and started towards the hallway, still so very familiar after all the intervening years. He paused in the arch that served at the doorway between the kitchen and the dining room. The dining table was filled with papers: receipts, files, bills. Susan clearly did not eat there. He turned and looked back. "You know, I've been given a lot of different names by a lot of different people. Been called a lot worse things than that." Susan looked over at him as she twisted the top off the jar of sauce. "Maybe I am half-man, half-critter. Who knows?"

"Ha," Susan snorted. "Return of the Goatman." She shot him a tender look. "'Return' being the operative word there, right?" She grabbed two potholders and reached for the large pot of noodles.

"Yeah." He nodded and glanced down at the floor. It was not the same floor as before, he realized. Before it had been black and white squares. Now it was a terracotta color. Susan dumped the noodles into a colander in the sink. It was suddenly too quiet, he thought. He glanced around him then. "Where are the girls?" He looked back at Susan.

She shot her eyes to one side to glance at him without moving her head. "Cleo is a freshman at Eastern, Robert. Cassie went to community college, made a nurse." She put the pan back on the stove and turned again to face him. "Works at a clinic over in Paint Lick. The 'girls' are grown up, Robert. They're not girls anymore. They're women. Strong, smart, brave women I'm damned proud of."

Robert let his eyes drift towards the sunlight that caught his eye from the window, looking unfocused at the beam filtering through the lacy curtain. A few motes swirled in the light, moved by the simple forces of light and breathing.

They had grown up. Of course they had. Now Susan was raising and lowering the colander to get the last few drops of water out. She let the colander fall one last time towards the sink and on the rise moved the drainer with its steaming mound of pasta across from the sink to the pot again. She didn't look up this time. "Go get cleaned up. This will keep a few minutes." She poured sauce into the noodles and stirred with the wooden spoon.

Robert returned, clean-shaven and scrubbed. It was his first hot shower in longer than he could remember. He did allow himself to luxuriate in it a bit, letting the steamy water pour against him. He loved the woods, the wildlife around him. He had found refuge there. But a hot shower was a delight that made civilization worth it.

Now Susan was on the back porch, sweeping up the trimmings from his haircut. He watched her work the broom. She had that same graceful movement he remembered, perhaps from all those years of dance lessons their mother had taken her to as a child. "You do that well," he grinned at her.

"Yeah, well, too much practice." She didn't look up. She swept the cuttings into a dustpan and carried them over to her raised garden bed and began shaking the clumps of hair across the dirt where already small green shoots were showing in neat rows. "One good thing, Robert. All that hair? It'll keep the rabbits out of my lettuce."

"Glad I could help." He glanced down and saw the bistro table had plastic placemats and stainless utensils placed on it. "Oh, al fresco, huh? I've done that a good deal lately."

Susan looked blankly at him. She had no idea how he had been living, he realized. For all she knew, he might have been sleeping in some flophouse on skid row in some city. Funny, he thought, how much he assumed people knew when they had no way of knowing.

Susan turned and walked to the garage, put away the broom and dustpan, and stepped up onto the porch. "It's a nice day for eating outside." She looked at him and set a thin smile. "No, it's a great day. My brother came home. My Robert is home."

He stepped aside from the doorway, and she came inside. She stopped to give him a hug and he wrapped his long arms around her and hugged her back. "You smell much better." Then she marched to a sink in a laundry room turned half-bath that Robert did not recall being there before. "Besides," she said, lathering her hands under the running water, "my dining table is out of control."

"Yeah, so I see." He looked through the kitchen towards the table. Even from two rooms away, the pile was clear. "What's that about?"

Susan dried her hands. "Well, there's bills and taxes and such. And Dad's house. We sold it. Lots of paperwork." Robert blinked. Another adjustment. Susan walked into the kitchen and took down a huge bowl from the cabinet. "And your house."

"You sold my house?" Robert felt a bile suddenly rise within him.

"No. No. I didn't. But that didn't mean I did nothing. I paid the taxes on it every year for one." She spooned a great mound of the mixture of pasta and sauce and broccoli into the bowl. "I have the total you owe me, by the way. And I have other stuff about it. Insurance, title, just stuff."

He processed that for a moment. Other stuff?

She handed him the bowl. Was this a serving bowl? "That's yours. See you on the veranda," she joked. She saw him gawking at the huge bowl of food. "You need a little meat on those bones."

He twisted his head in a gesture of, "Well, we'll see," then said, "Hell, Sis. I've been living like a hermit for, how long? Six years? I got no money to pay you with. Sorry." He raised an apologetic hand.

"Huh!" She grunted softly. "You do. Just don't know it." She filled a much smaller bowl that didn't match the pattern of his for herself and followed Robert to the porch.

Robert wondered what that might mean, but decided to wait to ask, at least until they had a chance to start eating. But it didn't make sense to him. He had left a bit of money in his checking account, sure, if that was even still active, and had he still been being paid? Maybe a few accounts had been outstanding, but not so many as to be remarkable. And his checking account wouldn't have earned any interest. No, he really was probably nearly as poor as he had been living for years.

He put the bowl down, sat, and began eating. It was a simple dish, but it was as satisfying as if he were at a banquet table. The salty noodles, the gooey sauce, the bite of the broccoli made for an extravagant meal, for him at least. And eating off an actual plate, using a fork, made him feel like some wild man being taken before the queen as an oddity. Just this much civilization was new, took some getting used to.

He realized he was shoveling the food into his mouth and made a conscious decision to slow down. He wasn't hiding. He wasn't living amongst the forest trees anymore. After his first few large mouthfuls, he put his fork down and paused, gathering himself. He looked over at Susan, who was stabbing a piece of broccoli. "I have money? Okay, but not much, though, right?"

"No, actually a lot." Susan sat straight, eating small forkfuls of the meal. He blinked at her, trying to follow. "Okay, you had whatever you had before, right?" He nodded. "Then when we sold Dad's place, we divided the money. You got that. I put it in your account. We each got a tidy sum."

"Why didn't you take the taxes out of that?" He enjoyed another bite, then put his fork down, continuing his deliberate return to society.

"Not how it works, Robert. I'm not taking your money. I

loaned it to you. You have to pay it back."

He nodded. "Okay."

"Plus, then you got the insurance money." She said it with a kind of finishing flourish.

He froze. "What insurance money?"

"From Bobby. I don't know exactly how much, but it was a lot. I think Bobby had maxed out what he could purchase." She waved with her fork. "Jean over at the bank? She's not really supposed to tell me, but, she says you got over half a million dollars in there." She stirred her bowl of pasta nonchalantly, as if she had just told him where to find a jar of peanut butter in the pantry.

Robert leaned forward and his eyes bulged from his face. "What?"

"Yeah, came in not long after you took off." She was enjoying this, he could tell.

Robert looked out in the yard. A rabbit hopped into the raised bed. "Be damned," he muttered. Now he looked back at his sister, who could not suppress a grin. "So, the house?"

Susan looked back quickly at her bowl, the smile disappearing quickly. "Yeah, about the house." She stabbed absently at her food. "The house is fine, as far as I can tell. From the outside, anyway. I drive by." She gave a shrug.

"Drive by? You still have a key, right?"

"Yeah." She diverted her eyes. She paused, weighing her words. "There's something you need to know about the house, Robert." Now she looked up through her bangs at him.

"Yes?" He sat motionless, waiting.

"You have company, it seems."

He blinked. "Company?"

"Yeah. Actually, squatters."

Chapter 4

"**S**quatters?" Robert lowered his fork and stared at Susan, blinked again, slowly, then stared some more. He was frozen for a moment, his hand holding the utensil that had a glop of pasta on it poised two inches above the bowl. She didn't look up, focused a bit overmuch on her small plate of food. He managed to find his thoughts. "What do you mean 'squatters?'"

Now she looked up and met his gaze, her face set in a stolid pose, gathering strength for what she was about to say. "Squatters, as in someone moved into your house while you were gone. 'Derelict property' I believe is the term." Her tone was vaguely accusatory, and Robert found himself put off by it. It wasn't as if he intended to have a derelict property, whatever that meant exactly. Or did he? Just now, he couldn't decide, and maybe he didn't have to reconcile all that. It was still his house, wasn't it? His and Bobby's. His stomach tightened. He laid the fork down in the bowl. He had been derelict; there was no denying that, but the house shouldn't have been. Wasn't that where family came in?

"So, what, a bunch of druggies moved in my house, and you just let them?" He waved both of his long hands in a kind of surrender.

Susan put her fork down as well and cocked her head to one side, curious. "Beg your pardon?" But that was no question.

Her brown eyes were piercing. "Did you ask me to take care of your property when you left? Oh, no, you didn't. And you know why you didn't? Because, in fact, you didn't even say goodbye. You never even told me you were leaving. You were gone two weeks before I even knew it. You walked away and left us here to hold the bag and now you're going to act as if I was supposed to take care of your life too?" Now her eyes were wide with anger. "Well, excuse me, Robert. Excuse me for having my own life to live, my own children to raise, my own house to take care of, my own job to go to, my own set of problems dealing with Dad that I had to work on day in and day out all by myself, because Daryl moved to the city and you disappeared like some sort of will-of-the wisp into the forest, and now, you want to know why I didn't take care of your property?" She waved her hands next to her head. Her voice had risen an octave as she spoke. Now she stood suddenly and picked up her barely touched plate of food. "Well, excuse me, Your Royal Highness, but I was just a tad busy." She pushed back the chair with the back of her legs, and it tilted over and banged against the wooden floor of the porch with a clatter. She winced. "Know what? I'm not hungry anymore."

She turned and walked back inside, leaving the overturned chair where it was. Robert sat there and blinked. He realized how badly he had reacted, and, no, it wasn't at all her fault. He looked down at the bowl of food. It smelled wonderful. He stood, walked around the table, and up-righted the chair, then picked up his bowl and followed Susan into the house. He took a forkful of food as he walked. It was such a welcome meal.

He walked through the house, eating as he went. Susan was scraping her plate back into the pot of pasta, saving it for another meal. She had ever been frugal, but being on her own had helped her learn to not waste anything. He himself had learned that in the wild. Or maybe he always knew that. Maybe it was their parents, Depression-era kids who knew better than to take anything for granted, who had taught this to them. Yes, it was just one thing they shared.

He paused in the doorway, watching her put the top on

the pot of pasta and rinsing her plate. He continued eating for a moment. Susan ignored him.

"I'm sorry," he finally managed. "No, it wasn't your responsibility." He scraped the sauce from the bottom of the bowl, realizing he had actually eaten the entire huge portion she had given him. "I was just surprised. I'm sorry," he said again.

Susan looked up from the sink now, her face softened by his apology. She set her lips and that was as much absolution as he would get, he figured, but he knew the look. He would have to accept it.

She reached her hand out for his bowl. "Want some more?" Okay, that felt more like forgiveness.

Robert managed a smile. "No, thank you. I feel like a snake that has swallowed a rat twice his size. I'm waiting for the bulge to show." She smirked, then took his bowl and rinsed it in the steaming water. He waited a moment, then asked, "Who moved into my house?"

Susan turned off the water and dried her hands on a dishtowel that at one time had a print on it, that now only hinted at once having been a picture. She turned and leaned back familiarly against the counter. She waited a second, evidently still dowsing her embers of anger from the porch.

"Okay, they aren't 'druggies,' as far as I can tell. It's a couple and their two kids." Susan put her hands behind her on the edge of the Formica countertop she was leaning against. "Don't know where they came from. I think she is a helper at a daycare center." Robert nodded, taking it in, trying to picture these people in his house. "He is maybe working at the prison?" She squinted in doubt. "Not sure." Now she walked over to the fridge, opened the door, and put the pot of leftover noodles inside. She grabbed two plastic bottles of water and turned back around, handing one to Robert. "Boy looks to be about seven. Little girl is maybe four or five." She gave a slight shrug. "They seem clean, normal." Robert realized Susan had been far more engaged with the situation than he had given her credit for. "No dog that I can tell, so that's good."

35

"You like dogs." Robert followed Susan as she led them past the table full of receipts and files. They went into the living room. The curtains were different. No, it was more than that. The entire window treatment was different. What had it been before? Valances? And where was her dog? *Chauncy*, he remembered. She had named him after the character in *Being There*. Cute little mutt.

"Yes, but a dog can be hard on a house, especially if people let it go in and out a lot." Susan sat in a wingback chair that Robert recognized from his parents' house. He sat on the couch. That at least was familiar. But everything about relaxing in his sister's house seemed utterly foreign to him. He had sat on logs and rocks and, more often than not, his haunches for so many years, a soft couch with throw pillows embroidered with pictures of Paris was downright awkward. True, his height had always made him a bit uncomfortable on normal people's furniture, but this was more. He didn't belong. Or at least, he didn't belong back, yet.

"True." He nodded, opened the bottle, and drank deeply the cold, clear water. It tasted like water he had drunk from a spring at the edge of a trail far up on a mountain, in the Tetons, maybe. "Where's Chauncy?" He glanced around.

Susan shook her head. "We lost Chauncey a couple of years ago." He felt another jab in his solar plexus.

When he looked back at his sister, she was watching him, almost studying him. "I can't believe you're here, Robert," she finally managed. "Truth is, I worried about you. A lot."

Robert looked down at the floor now. "I'm sorry."

"I know. I know." Her voice had softened. He could hear the familiar slight rasp in her tone. Then she added, as if to say, "enough of that," "You need to go see Martin."

"Martin?" Robert looked up.

"Martin Douglas. He handled Mom's stuff, and Dad's, when we sold it."

"Oh, lawyer." He leaned forward and put the water bottle on the little coffee table, then pressed his fingertips together.

"Yeah." Susan leaned forward and put a coaster under his

bottle. "He's good. I asked him about it. They can't really claim your house. If they had paid taxes and such, they might have a claim, but, like I say, I paid those." Robert nodded, watching Susan curl her slender legs up familiarly on the family chair.

"Okay. I will. I'll make an appointment right now," he said resolutely, and looked around him. "Where's the phone?" He leaned forward.

Susan laughed. "Well, today's Saturday, so he won't be in, and I don't have a phone in the house anymore." He looked at her quickly. She reached behind her and pulled out a cell phone. She wriggled it back and forth, as if he had perhaps never seen one before.

"Okay, but you HAD a phone. We couldn't get any coverage down here." He tried to defend his question.

"They put a tower over on Jimmy Barlow's place. Good coverage now."

"Huh." He tried to picture it.

"No sense paying for two phones, the way I see it." She put the phone back into her hip pocket.

"No, guess not." So many changes, Robert thought. "Wait, on top of the hill there? By the pond?"

"Yeah, 'fraid so." But her tone was not sorry.

Such was the price of civilization, he guessed, and everyone just accepted it unquestioningly. All those memories. He paused, recalling those happy summer days so very many years ago. He looked off into the past for a moment, then back at Susan, who watched him carefully, letting him wander back in time. "So," he started.

"No, not a word."

"What?"

"You were going to ask about Nikki, right?" He stared at his sister a second. "You don't think I knew?" She grinned at him. He looked at his hands, suddenly too large for his sister's house. "Robert?" Her voice was softer now, revealing the scratchiness again. He looked up in response but didn't speak. Her grin was replaced now with a sympathetic smile. "Where you been?"

He paused just a second, then he leaned back and told his sister about his journey, how at first he had simply wanted to take a walk to clear his head. Then he decided to camp a bit, commune with the forest the way he and Bobby had so many times. He told her how it had felt good to be away from the sad, sympathetic nods from well-meaning friends and acquaintances, so he had decided to go farther into the woods, as if going into the trees might somehow make the reality of it all go away.

Susan listened intently. She did not interrupt, but nodded her understanding ever so slightly, as a maple might sway gently in a summer breeze. And then, he told her, he began walking farther and farther and the journey took on a life of its own and how he had welcomed that, glad that the journey had its own kind of life force and that energy had propelled him to follow game paths deep into the mountains and to trace rivers back down into the plains. He told her about the occasional truck ride when he found himself too near a town, the drivers always surprised when he asked to be let off on the edge of the farthest reaches.

"In fact," Robert said, smiling, "one guy literally said to me as he was pulling off into some parking area on the interstate, 'Buddy, this ain't nowhere,' and I told him, 'Ever think that except for one tiny space, *Nowhere* is the same as *Now Here*?'" Robert laughed at the memory. Susan gave him a grin, but she didn't comment. "I met people. At least at first. There was a woman." He looked up at Susan to see her reaction. Susan's eyes widened in interest. "Karen."

Susan tilted her head as if to say, "And?"

"I liked her. She was nice." He paused and looked off, out the window, at a memory several years in the past. "Huh," he grunted after a moment. "She hated that word: 'nice.' She said it was the most overused, worthless word in the English language." Robert let his gaze return to Susan, who picked up her bottle and screwed off the top to take another swig of water. "Did you know *nice* originally meant *stupid*? Well, that's what she said." He shook his head slightly, then stared down at the rag rug on his sister's living room floor. "She left." He felt a small gloom come over him. "Just like everyone else." He let himself fall into the gloom for a second, such a familiar feeling, he almost seemed unclothed when he let it fall away. He stopped talking, allowing the feeling to creep up into him.

"I didn't," Susan finally said. He looked up at her and then he let himself climb out of the dark feeling.

"No, you didn't, did you?" He stood and stepped over to Susan's chair. She stood and they hugged again for a long time. Finally, he pulled back and looked down at her. "You know what?"

"What?" She looked up, her hands still locked behind his sinewy waist.

"You're my hero."

"Ha!" Susan burst out a laugh. She let go of him. "I'm no one's hero, I promise you." She glanced over at the dining table, out of control with paper.

He followed her eyes. "No, you are. You have done everything, all by yourself. You're strong and smart and, I don't know," he groped for the word, "determined."

"Well, if you mean stubborn as a crooked nail, then, yeah, I suppose I am." She stood with her hands on her thin waist, still sending glances at the table.

"That your files are a wreck does not mean a thing," he said. He stood next to her, looking at the stacks of receipts. "You know, there's a reason I came here first, Sis." She looked up at him. "You're my rock." He shrugged. She gave him a smile.

"Good."

"But that," he pointed at the table. "That is a mess." They both laughed. "How can I help?" He walked towards the table.

"No, I can do it."

"I'm willing to help." He raised his hands.

"No, actually, I have a method. Just leave it be."

"Method," he repeated, looking at the mounds of paper. "Okay." He looked back at Susan and paused, waiting for the thought to allow itself to form. "Maybe we could go see the house?"

Susan pressed her lips together. "You sure you want to do that?" That sounded more like a suggestion than a question.

"Yeah, I think so." He nodded.

"You can't get all angry with them, those folks in your house. You gotta stay calm. It won't help anything if you get mad."

"Me? Mad?" He held his hand to his chest and opened his eyes wide. "When have I ever lost my temper?"

Susan shot him a look. "Well, there was Charlie Jones." She started on a list, her fingers counting up.

"Oh no, that was way back in high school, and he was trying to move in on my girl." But he knew where this was going.

"You beat him up pretty bad, Robert. And then, there was Donnie Wilson," she continued, counting on another finger.

"But he was picking on Daryl and . . ." Then he paused. He had to admit, he had had a reputation of something of a quick temper. "Yeah." He nodded. "Maybe we can just drive by. If I go in . . ." He let it trail off.

"Yeah. Before you go over there all half-cocked, you need to talk with Martin. You'll feel better if you know what you need to know, you know?" Robert looked at his sister and they both chuckled at the awkward sentence she had uttered. "Well, you get the idea," she said. She walked over to the little marble-topped table by the door and picked up her keys.

Chapter 5

"Terry, won't you pour some milk for the kids?" The woman looked at herself in the hazy mirror. They had found the rusty vanity on the side of the road and the silvering had pretty much worn off the back of the mirror, but it was just as well. She didn't know why she bothered to look. She wasn't very happy with what she saw whenever she did: pudgy cheeks, sagging bags around her eyes, more chins than anyone was supposed to have. At least it was only a vanity mirror and not full-length. The squeals of two children screaming at each other was almost a welcome call away from the scene she was seeing. Almost.

She spun towards the door of the little bathroom. "Terry?" she called out as she reached for the dented brass knob. She walked into the hallway and glanced into the bigger of the two bedrooms, the one she and her husband shared. He was sprawled across the bed, still sleeping. The shrieks from the kitchen propelled her to continue without rousing him. How he could sleep through the racket was beyond her comprehension.

In the kitchen, her two children sat in resin, stackable lawn chairs at the metal dining table, the hair on both their heads tousled and filled with the various colors of the sugary cereal they had begged for at the grocery. Cereal was everywhere, across the table, on the floor, strewn across the old used stove behind the boy.

The boy and girl did not pause from the food fight, even when she walked in, exasperated, so tired of screaming kids. A spray of syrupy scented cereal flew into her face, a poor shot from the little girl towards her brother.

Suddenly, the mother's head was pounding. "Stop it," she yelled as loudly as she could. God, she hoped that woke up Terry. The children stopped throwing food, but they sat there, giggling, looking at each other, grinning. The mother took a deep breath. "This is why we buy Rainbow Blossom Cereal? So you can throw it all over the kitchen? Look at this." She splayed her hands out in front of her. "Look at this," she said again, more loudly, when they didn't bother to look. The kids did look this time but did not seem impressed. But the boy at least sensed her frustration.

"Sorry, Mom," he tossed her way. He reached for the box, which had to be nearly empty by now.

"No," the mother snatched the box from his hands. "You've had yours. These are mine." She hated the god-awful things, but there was no way the two of them were getting any more. She plopped the box on the countertop, away from the kids, next to the stained, empty drip coffee maker. "You think this stuff grows on trees?" The two kids looked at her now with a bit of despair, their sugar rush needing a refill. Her daughter seemed to be considering just where Rainbow Blossom Cereal grew.

"Mommy?" Rose asked. "Wouldn't Rainbow Blossoms have to grow on Rainbow Flowers?" She cocked her head to one side.

Charlene let her arms drop to her side. "I don't know, honey. I guess so."

"Let's plant some," Rose grinned. It was hard to tell if she was serious. Her imagination was so overactive.

Terry stumbled from the hallway and leaned against the door facing. He was wearing the same boxer shorts and stretched-out tee shirt he had slept in.

"You make coffee?" he mumbled, rubbing the stubble on his chin.

The woman shook her head. "For God's sake, Terry, put

42

some clothes on."

"Man can't walk around in his own house in his underwear?" He shuffled over to the coffee maker and pulled out the pot. He saw there was no coffee yet, so he shoved the carafe back in. He picked up the cereal box and dug out a handful of the nasty mix and shoved it in his mouth. He walked to the table and started pouring cereal into the girl's bowl. The mother looked at him in disbelief.

"Fine, you clean it up." She threw up her hands, turned, and started towards the door to the hallway. She stopped in the doorway to turn and shake her head disapprovingly at her motley family.

This was even worse than the mirror. At least she could get away from the mirror.

"What's all the yelling about?" Terry asked the boy as he emptied the box into his bowl.

"We was playin', is all." The boy watched his father walk over now to the round-fronted refrigerator and retrieve the plastic milk carton. His bare feet crunched on pastel marshmallow chunks. He didn't seem to notice. The mother threw up her hands and walked into the small living room. She could hear the cereal crunching underfoot as her husband went back across the kitchen.

"Well, get the broom, Luke. Rosie, get the dustpan. Y'all sweep it all up."

She heard the chairs scooting. She gave out a sigh. At least he was getting them to clean it up.

She stood on the carpet remnant on the floor of the living room, letting them get the job done. She hated to admit it, but Terry's calmness had handled the situation better than she had. "No, Rosie," she heard Terry say slowly. "Don't eat it. It's been on the floor, honey. You can't eat it no more." The woman managed a small smile. She imagined her little girl gobbling down the dusty remnants of sugary trash food. She didn't know any better. But as she let her mind's eye wander, she glanced out the large multi-paned window.

"Terry?" she called.

"Yeah, babe?" Terry came into the room. She could hear the coffee maker gurgling in the kitchen.

"That woman's back." She stared out the window. Terry approached the window and rearranged himself exaggeratedly. He did not look out, especially, just in the direction of the window. He knew the scene.

"Huh," he snorted. "Hope she likes the view." He cupped himself through his boxers.

"Terry," she barked softly. "Stop that." But she would have to admit, she found it amusing. It would serve the woman right. She wished she would stop patrolling their house.

Yes, she knew who she was. She was the sister of the man who had built the house. But he was gone, right? Nobody even knew where he was. He wasn't using it. What harm was there if she and Terry and the kids lived here? An empty house can just fall apart. Houses need people, the way she saw it. Besides, they had added things to the house. Sure, they were mostly cast-offs, the rusty vanity for one, and the used refrigerator, since the other one had been grown over on the inside with mold and had had to be carted off to the dump, liquefied produce and reeking mysterious globs of leftovers still in it. Terry told her later, when he took the door off at the dump, how awful it had been, even worse than the stench of the dump itself. They were doing him a favor, weren't they? Sort of? Well, that was how she chose to think about it, although it was true Terry talked about how they could claim ownership at some point, but she wasn't exactly clear how that worked.

"Okay, Charlene, but she needs to mind her own business." He turned now, but he certainly did not seem to be in any hurry to cover himself from the view of the window. Charlene continued to stare out the window at the little hatchback parked just up the road.

"Terry?" she said finally. Terry turned and faced her, his face noncommittal. "Someone else in the car too." Now Terry turned and leaned towards the window, peering out.

"Is that so?" he murmured. Then after a pause, he added, in a voice meant to not be heard from the kitchen, "Think it's the sheriff?" Charlene heard the tiniest edge in his tone. Now he stood to one side and draped the curtain over the lower part of his body. He studied the car parked up the hill, just beyond the mulberry tree.

"Don't think so." Charlene walked over to Terry and leaned out from behind him, as if she too were hiding from view, although she at least had on sweatpants and a baggy sweater. It was as if she were using him for a shield should gunfire suddenly blast through the window. "Sheriff is a short little guy. That person looks like their head's scraping the roof."

"Yeah," Terry said absently, still appraising the car atop the hill. Then he turned, pulled the curtain towards the middle, and looked at her. He didn't say a word and he didn't need to. She thought the same thing at the same moment, and she felt her stomach do a quick flip. There was a second of sudden silence. Even the children were quiet, as if the moment called them to be.

"What do we do, Terry?" she said finally and swallowed hard.

He looked at her for just a moment, his mind working it over she could tell, then nodded. "Same thing we always do," he said matter-of-factly. She looked at him, trying to decide if it was a riddle. He saw the look on her face, so he added, "We just do the things we always do. If you were going shopping today, go ahead and go. Kids can help me on the garden. We just act like it's any other Saturday." He shrugged. "We just be normal. Hell, Charlene, we are normal. He's the one, from what I hear, ain't normal. Done run off and left everything." He jerked his thumb towards the window. Charlene looked doubtfully at the closed curtain. Terry stepped next to her and put an arm around her shoulder. "Go get some coffee, Darling. Pour me a cup? I'm gonna get dressed."

She looked at him now, her heart not pounding as badly as it had a moment ago. Sometimes his calmness drove her nuts, but sometimes she found great relief in it. This was a relief time. He let go of her shoulder and she walked back into the kitchen. The floor was mostly clear of cereal, although a few pale pink and blue tidbits were over by the backdoor. The children were happily munching away, Luke reading the cereal box, Rosie staring off at nothing, simply enjoying the sweetness in her mouth.

"What might happen" scared Charlene almost every day. Her Momma told her she should find a job as a professional worrier because it was the one thing she was naturally gifted at. She took down two mismatched mugs, one advertising a bank in Huntington, the other extolling the drinker as The World's Best Grandad. She poured the dark, bitter liquid in, added creamer powder to hers in the bank cup, then turned to the kids.

Rosie still had a pale green marshmallow rainbow in her dark curls. Charlene shook her head, took her cup, and sat at the table next to Rosie. Her resin chair had a crack in the side she knew to avoid so it wouldn't pinch her. She reached over and retrieved the cereal bit from her hair. Rosie simply turned and looked at her without emotion, as if having food taken from her hair at the breakfast table was the most ordinary thing in the world.

She loved these kids something fierce. It was maybe the one thing she had gotten right in her life. The kids and Terry. Yes, they drove her crazy, but they were also her pride and joy, as she told her co-workers at Happy B's DayCare. She loved telling Frankie, and especially Bonnie, the owner, all about the kids. She usually left out the parts about family arguments and when the kids fought. All kids bicker, she reasoned. That wasn't worth talking about. But her little girl's beautiful graduation from kindergarten was definitely an item to share, complete with photos on her old cell phone. The women had ooh-ed and aww-ed appropriately too.

What would happen to them, her precious babies, if they had to leave the house? All memory of the pounding headache from the screeching kids before receded now with an actual threat. Now, she really did have something to worry about.

She took the tiniest pleasure in actually having a real concern, something to fret about that was in front of them, not simply a "what-if worry," as Terry called it.

It was only because they had found this place, abandoned and sad-looking, needing a family in it, that they were able to make ends meet. No, the house wasn't perfect. The countertops were not the right height, being a good four inches too tall for her. There were only the two bedrooms. She wished the kids had their own room. Terry had floated the idea of adding another little room off the back some day for Luke to sleep in. She wasn't crazy about his being away from the rest of them when they slept, but the promise of it helped calm her concerns, at least for a while. And the house was awfully small for the four of them in other ways, with the front porch bigger than the living room, and only one bathroom and just a shower in that, rather than a tub. But Terry said the house was solid, the plumbing was good, there was some land around it, and, best of all, they weren't paying any rent.

"Thanks, Darling." Terry came in dressed in worn-out Dickey work pants and a long-sleeved plaid cotton shirt that had once been her daddy's, rest his soul. It was his usual work-in-the-garden clothes. He picked up his cup and took a gulp, grimacing slightly at the heat of it, before taking another gulp, this time slurping in air to cool it as he drank it. He put the cup on the countertop and turned to the table. "Luke, Rosie, go get dressed. Put on your jeans. We got a garden to dig." Luke rolled his eyes, put down the cereal box, and scooted back from the table. He turned to sulk away. "Wait," Terry said.

The boy turned, looked back, then went and picked up his bowl, emptied the pinkish milk into the sink, and ran water into it. Rosie half-scooted the chair she was in, half-slid out. She grabbed her bowl, clearly happy to have somewhat remembered to do what her brother had forgotten. She pranced over to the sink, the bowl at a forty-five-degree angle, milk dribbling the entire trip, and let the bowl drop with a clatter into the sink.

Terry watched her and smiled. He gave a nod to Charlene

that it was okay about the trail of milk: he would get it.

Charlene changed into a pair of slacks and her favorite white pullover sweatshirt. It really wasn't cold enough for the sweatshirt, but she was always chilly, and the Wal-Mart always made her teeth chatter, they kept it so cold. She was glad Terry was off this weekend. She did not love bringing the kids to the store. They always whined about wanting something and pouted or even threw a tantrum if they didn't get it, which she almost always did, her resistance worn down by their persistence.

Plus, they were starting in on the garden. She loved watching things grow that they could eat. It satisfied something deep within her to have at least a semblance of self-reliance. She had to admit, she even rather enjoyed the weeding, unless it got out of control. When she had driven their old Hyundai out of the dusty dirt drive, that woman in the car was gone. She was very glad about that. Maybe it was nothing. Maybe it wasn't the man whose house it was, returned now from God knows where. Charlene made up her mind to take as much time as she liked at the store. As much as she hated going to the giant box store, it was just about the closest thing she had to time for herself anymore.

Two hours later, Charlene puttered the little sedan up to the house, the back seat and the small cargo area behind it filled with plastic shopping bags. She hated taking so many trips with all the bags, but she disliked it even more when the bags were too full and they pulled tight, cutting into her fingers as she wagged them into the house.

On her trips back and forth, she saw Terry and the kids out in the garden patch. It was the same patch as last year, of course, and turning it was made easier by that; that and the fact that Terry was good at composting the coffee grounds and eggshells and various vegetable matter and turning the compost pile every so often. It took her three trips to the car, the last one a bit overloaded but manageable.

Through the wavy kitchen door window, she could watch them finishing up the work while she unloaded the groceries.

Terry had his shirt off, and his slightly pudgy body glistened with sweat as he turned spade after spade of dirt. Luke followed behind, chopping up the dirt clods with the hoe. Rosie was at the back of the row, awkwardly pushing and pulling a too-long garden rake.

Charlene smiled a blessing upon them. Then she turned and finished unloading. She had gotten more Rainbow Blossom cereal for the kids. She hoped they had gotten the wastefulness out of them this morning. She had also gotten a six-pack of Bud Light for Terry. They didn't often keep beer in the house, more because they had such a tight budget than anything else, but for some reason, this weekend it seemed appropriate, what with that nagging feeling from the woman in the car and whoever that was with her. Plus, she had gotten some new face cream for herself, so she wanted to balance the scales a bit.

She finished putting it all away, which took some extra time at the end since there really was not enough cabinet space for the boxes and cans of food they usually ate, and it became a game of Tetris at the end. Her family tromped onto the back porch and leaned the tools against the post of the shed roof. All three of them were covered in dirt and wet with sweat. She heard Terry telling them to take off their shoes before coming in. Luke half-trudged, half-ambled in, looking perpetually bored. He had smears of dirt on his right cheek and his pant legs were muddy up to his knees. If he was a reluctant worker, he was at least obedient. "Go get a shower," she told him. "And put your clothes in the basket."

He rolled his eyes and muttered, "Okaaay," resignedly.

"I'm making sandwiches, and I got some cheese puffs. Be ready when you are all clean," she called after him as he made his way down the hall, but in truth, the cheese puffs were more Rosie's treat than his. But the bologna, sliced American cheese, and mustard on white bread was his favorite, so it was all equal.

Rosie came in and Charlene handed her a bright green metal glass of water, which she began gulping down. She handed Terry a beer when he came in afterwards, having put his shirt back on. He grinned his approval and Charlene basked just a bit in it. She gave him a broad smile.

"Daddy?" Rosie gasped just a bit, lowering the cup now from her first heavy drink.

"Yes, sweetie?" Terry popped the top of the beer and took a long, slow drink.

"Who was that man?"

Charlene spun and looked down at her daughter, and Terry took the beer away from his mouth so quickly, some of it dripped down his chin.

"What man, Rosie?"

Their daughter looked up at her daddy, her eyes wide with innocence. "The one in the woods." Now she took another drink, but less frantically. Terry looked at Charlene, his eyes wide too, but with concern. He put his beer on the counter and squatted down next to Rose.

"What did the man look like, Rosie?"

"I don't know. He was kind of a giant."

Terry looked up at Charlene, then back at his daughter. "A giant. Huh. Where was the man?" Charlene could hear the barely suppressed anxiety in his voice. His shirt was already moist from working in the sun earlier, but this didn't seem to be helping.

"In the woods," she was matter of fact about it. "Over by the swing." Charlene pictured the tree where Terry had tied the heavy rope to the oak, an old tire tied to the bottom as a swing.

"What was he doing, darling?" Charlene thought Terry might be pouring on the "everything is okay" routine a bit thick, but she herself certainly wasn't helping, just standing there frozen.

"Nothing." Rosie took another drink of water. "He just stood there. He looked like a tree." She giggled at herself. "He was a giant," she said in mock seriousness.

"Oh, he's not a giant. He's just a neighbor, checking in on us," Terry lied. Now he stood, looked again at Charlene, and picked up his beer. Charlene considered opening one for herself, but she hated the way beer made her feel all bloated. "Go take a shower when Lukie gets out."

"Okay." Rose put the nearly empty cup on the counter and headed for the hallway.

"Mommy'll be right there, Rosie," Charlene called after her, her "everything is okay" voice not nearly as convincing as Terry's. She looked at her husband and swallowed hard. Terry looked in her direction, but he wasn't seeing her. His mind was focused far away.

Chapter 6

Susan pulled the comforter up on the bed and straightened it. She tossed the two pillows she used and along the top placed the two with the decorative shams that she had moved to the armchair for the night. That would suffice as "made," she decided, but it looked neat, tidy, so she was happy with it.

She walked down the hallway and into the dining room where she had stayed up until three, sorting and resorting the papers, trying to force some sort of coherence on them. Although the later she worked, the less certain she was of the categories she had been using earlier in the night, so she found herself going back through already piled up receipts and moving them into fewer and fewer stacks. But the table looked better. She had managed to reduce it to three neat piles, each one held down by whatever weight was handy. Then, energized by the task being completed, she had read the novel she had picked up at the library she had started last week for another thirty minutes, before finally getting her eyelids heavy enough for sleep.

She surveyed her work from the previous night. Beneath the covered candy dish partially filled with individually wrapped mints were the papers from selling their father's house: title, transfer, taxes, sales contract, and so forth. She would find a manila folder today and squirrel them away in the file cabinet, in the added-on family room, in case she ever needed them again, which she seriously doubted. They had been on her table quite long enough.

Under the saucer with the cinnamon-scented candle were the bills she needed to write out payments for today, so she could mail them out tomorrow. The checkbook and a give-away pen from someone named Alex Carson, who ran for county court clerk unsuccessfully, despite the various pieces of swag handed out door to door, lay next to them. She would write the checks and stuff the envelopes today and mail them out tomorrow, when the post office opened. She needed stamps.

She still didn't quite trust doing the checks on-line through the bank. There were so many security breaches going on: what if someone got into her bank account? She only had so much money. Finally, under the desk stapler from her job at the insurance agency, were the bills already paid. She was waiting only for the cleared checks to confirm. Then she would place them too in a folder, in the file cabinet. Her friend Ellie who did her books told her she could toss them after a year if they weren't tax related, but the years of gathered cancelled checks in the drawer was evidence enough that would likely not happen.

She paused before the table long enough to admire her work from the previous night. Robert's return had motivated her to get things straightened up, perhaps as much from being embarrassed by the clutter as anything, but she decided that didn't matter, as long as she got it done. Motivation was good, she decided, regardless of its source. Next on her mental list was the basement, but that was a much bigger task.

She went into the kitchen where Mr. Coffee was turning the remnants of a pot into a bitter, dark ink. It had clearly been cooking far too long. The kitchen reeked of burnt coffee. She glanced up at the clock. Ten fifteen. She had slept late, after staying up until the wee hours. She guessed Robert had made the pot of coffee, but what time had he gotten up? And where was he? It amazed her he could not smell the ruined coffee.

She turned off the hotplate and started making a fresh pot. As she put clean water in the carafe, she glanced out the window above the sink. She saw her tall brother's seemingly disembodied head gliding along the top of a plank fence as he strolled up towards the back gate. It was the opposite side of the street.

Out back was only the lane that became a country road a mile or less away. There was nothing out there but cows and cornfields, and then woodlands that stretched up into the mountains not far off. She reached up, suddenly a little shaky, and turned the water off from filling the coffee pot. She braced herself momentarily on the edge of the sink.

It occurred to her if he wandered out there away from everyone, he might be tempted to head back out into the forest, to disappear again. She felt herself make an earnest hope, almost a prayer, if she believed in such things, that he would stay, that he would not grow weary so quickly of being around people, well, around her, since no one else even knew he was back.

But who did know? He clearly had been out walking in plain sight, if out on the edge of the city limits. And he had gone for a walk yesterday as well, which she only discovered when he came in the side gate while she was sowing zinnias along the edge of the walkway she had fashioned from found pavers. Of course, he was accustomed to being outside, and her own house would no doubt feel claustrophobic after so many years wandering the wilderness, as he had phrased it, the irony of his statement not lost on her. And it was not like he needed to be in hiding, at least, not anymore.

But if absolutely anyone saw him, it would be all over town in a matter of minutes. News of Robert Younger's return would be big. Once anyone at The Flintrock Grille heard about it, it would be like the siren for the volunteer firemen going off. Everyone would know. Not that that was bad. It wasn't. He had been an important part of the community, once upon a time. He had led the Boy Scout troop through several different populations, the boys moving on to adulthood, replaced by younger brothers, cousins, acquaintances. Everyone in Wyler's Ford knew each other, and most were related in some fashion. It was both the best thing and the worst thing about her hometown, to Susan. Robert was also on the search and rescue team that occasionally got called out when students from the university got lost in the national forest or, much worse, when they fell from the cliffs around the gorge, all too often because they were high on something or simply careless and youthful, where carelessness and perceived invincibility could be deadly. He regularly participated, and usually won, the turkey shoots held on Founder's Day every August.

Everyone knew Robert and everyone liked him. Well, mostly everyone. What harm would it do if others knew that he was back, she didn't know. Maybe she just wanted him to herself for a bit longer. But she at least wanted him to talk with Martin before the squatters knew he was there. Maybe the element of surprise somehow weighed in his favor. She didn't know. But if it was a resource, it was only available if she kept him home, at her house. Safe.

She would have to admit that at least a part of her hoarding her brother was to protect him. There had been many bad rumors, disparaging comments, idle talk of almost conspiracy level issues. She hated all of it. They were wrong to talk badly about Robert. He was a good man going through the hardest time. But people just can't help but pick at the corpse of a memory they once held dear, if for no other reason it confirmed, if he wasn't as good a man as they once believed, maybe they hadn't lost so much if he was gone.

But she couldn't abide the sinister nature of the chatter and had at first chided people, then grown frustrated, and then angry, and finally she cursed out the client of the insurance agency when she said in mock whisper something about Robert being in what they so originally called "the looney bin" to her boss, but clearly with the mean-spirited intent of Susan hearing. She lost her job, since obsequiousness is evidently the hallmark of good business, and later lost friends, but she was not going to let them harm her brother, or even the memory of him. She would see to that.

She heard the back storm door clap shut, the pneumatic

door so worn-out there was nothing gentle about the action. It was on the list, her list, to replace that one day. Soon. She poured the water into the reservoir and flipped the switch for the coffeemaker.

Robert was a big man, but the floor joists barely grunted as he walked towards the kitchen. She wondered how he managed to be so quiet. She turned, and even though she, of course, had seen him, she was startled to see him there in the doorway, his head bent so he wouldn't bump it on the top of the doorway. Although he wouldn't, even if he straightened up and tried to. But Susan decided maybe tall people are always ducking, out of habit as much as anything, the same way she winced whenever she saw a bug in her house, half-expecting, half-dreading it to be a spider. Robert carried one of her several travel coffee cups, tall plastic containers with sippy-cup tops. He held it low, at an angle, clearly empty.

"Another pot percolating right now. Be ready in a jif." She gave him her best sisterly smile. She saw him glance at the machine. She sounded forced, even to herself. And she wondered why she said "percolating." It was a drip maker. She gave out a sigh, letting herself calm down a moment.

"I left the pot on. Thought you might be up soon," He stepped into the kitchen and straightened, walked over to the sink, and rinsed the cup. "Smells like I was wrong." His voice was hoarse, like he had not spoken in a long time. He put the cup on the drain board. Was that a "no" to more coffee?

"Nice walk?" Susan leaned against the counter. She wanted to think about anything other than Robert's leaving.

"Yeah." He turned and looked down at her, but he didn't elaborate. She wanted to ask where he had been, if he saw anyone, and thus had been seen, so she could expect the rumor mill to be at full-tilt. He was a strong man, a good brother, but his leaving had changed how she saw him, more fragile than she had ever dreamed. Not fragile like a butterfly's wings, the very touching of which threatened to ruin them. It was more like the fragility in the sense of safety she saw when, just a few mornings ago, she had watched the doe and her fawns, still with their spots, gamboling in the puddles. They were playful and carefree and whatever was the deer counterpart to happy, until she had leaned forward to enjoy watching them; and just that much movement had sent them high-tailing it across the lane and into the underbrush. It was as if she were waiting for him to high-tail into the underbrush. Perhaps that was her worst fear threatening to come true.

She looked up and realized she had been gazing out the windows, lost in her train of thought, and Robert had been satisfied to simply wait her out, wait for her to return from wherever she had gone. She tried to recall if he had always been this patient. It was like she was meeting him all over again. She knew him better than she knew almost anyone, but she knew nothing about him. The man could take down a bull elk and skin it before the elk knew what happened, but Susan saw how tenuous it all was, his coming back, his hometown so strange to him now, no doubt.

Wyler's Ford never changed, everyone said, but it did, if only subtly. People were getting older, the population in general, as the kids seemed to never come home from college or even the local trade school, both of which educated them for jobs that just didn't exist there. The only people she saw any more at the Piggly Wiggly were old people, well, people her age and older, not that she was old yet. But no young people older than the high schoolers who worked there for a year or two, then disappeared into the vapor of society writ large.

"Eggs?" She finally managed to bring herself back.

Robert gave her a wry smile. "What kind?"

Susan turned and looked at him, shook her head, and walked over to the fridge. "Osprey eggs, goofy." She pulled out the grey-white carton of eggs.

Robert gave out grunting sigh. "Never had those. Now goose eggs? That's a delicacy you should try, Sis." The coffee maker burbled its final spurts of water through the filter, and he reached for his cup he had washed. Even that little bit of his taking some comfort warmed Susan's thoughts.

"Yeah? Well, these are just plain old chicken eggs." She returned to the fridge and pulled out a plastic bag of bacon. She didn't always like the scent cooked bacon left, enticing when it was cooking, but lingering then for hours, but it had to be better than the rank first pot of coffee. She unwrapped the bacon and laid out the strips on the metal rack of a roasting pan. "So," she couldn't resist, "where'd you go on your walk?" She slid the pan in the oven and pushed buttons on the range top. She turned and looked at Robert. She had wanted to sound nonchalant, idly curious, but in wanting to sound any particular way, she always felt like she was as transparent as a dandelion seed.

"Church." Robert put the plastic lid on the cup. Susan wondered how long it might have been since he actually had a cup of coffee. She raised her eyebrows at his response. "Well, my church." He motioned towards the window with his chin. "It is Sunday." He shot her a mischievous grin.

"Yeah." Susan walked over to pull down a bowl from the cupboard, an old one that had been their grandmother's, Hall's Autumn Tea Leaves, but with most of the gold rim either worn off or chipped down to the porcelain. "See God?" she teased.

"Of course," he took a long drink of the coffee. It had to be scalding, she figured, but he didn't seem to care.

She nodded. "Of course," she echoed him. She started breaking the eggs into the bowl. "So, Robert?" she started. He didn't speak an answer, simply acknowledged the question with his attention. "Are you glad to be back?"

Robert broke into a grin. "Sis, words cannot describe how glad I am to be back, to see you, to feel, I don't know, ready to get back at it, my life."

Susan whisked the eggs, added some half-and-half in, and whisked some more. "I'm glad. I'm very glad." She paused.

"What?" He leaned back, curious.

"What?" she repeated. She pulled a cast iron skillet from the warming drawer under the oven. She wished she had been getting it heated already. She had grown unaccustomed to cooking for anyone else.

"There's something else you're not saying." Now his posture was perhaps a bit perturbed.

"It's nothing, Robert. Just one of my quirks."

"Quirks?" He took another drink from the coffee. Susan grabbed a mug and finally poured herself one while butter melted in the skillet.

"Yeah, so I've been thinking . . ."

"Uh oh."

She waved him off. "No, I've been thinking about the things people say. Some of them don't make any sense to me." She poured some of the half-and-half into her cup and stirred it.

"Such as?" His perturbed demeanor was gone now. It was just his kooky sister, was his manner now.

"Yeah." She took a long drink of coffee. "One of them is what you just said. 'Words cannot express.' It's a contradiction of its own terms. By saying that, you are expressing how much you feel it. Obviously, you can express it in words. And at the same time, it's an odd admission of a lack of your own vocabulary. Of course, there are words to express it. You just did." She felt herself get pulled into the little sermon she had rehearsed in her own thoughts a dozen times in mental discussions with Ellie or with Cleo, saving for when she came home from college in a few weeks, something to start a conversation with her daughter she could already feel being pulled away. She poured the eggs into the bubbling butter in the skillet. She went on with her train of thought. "Yet you feel compelled to say you simply don't have words, a better vocabulary. That's the part I don't get. For that matter, if someone cannot express something, why would they even try to convey a thought for which they are admittedly unable? Keep it to yourself. Go read a book. There's something like a hundred seventy thousand words in the English language. Go learn some of them, then tell me how you feel." She looked up from stirring the eggs at Robert, who was grinning now, amused at her little rant. "Sorry. Too much time on my hands."

Robert cocked his head then, a question occurring to him.

"You still work at the bank, Sis?" He took another drink of coffee.

"Bank?" She stirred the eggs some more. The scent of the bacon was beginning to overtake the odor of coffee. "No, I haven't worked there in years."

"Oh," Robert appeared to be mulling over the term "years."

"I worked at Bobby Lee's for a while." The eggs were beginning to set.

"Selling insurance?" His face wore a look of surprise.

"No, office stuff. Forms, claims, whatnot." She walked over to the cabinet and retrieved two white plates.

"Ah. 'For a while.' So, you're not there anymore?"

Susan suppressed the memory she had had just minutes before. She opened the oven door to check on the bacon. It needed a minute or two more. "You want toast?" She suddenly remembered toast, a way to change the subject in case Robert asked why she didn't work there still.

"No, I'm good. Bacon and eggs will be wonderful. Did you know peahen eggs taste just like a chicken egg?" Susan took relief her tactic worked.

"What's a peahen?" She spooned the eggs onto the plates.

"Girl peacock." Robert started opening drawers, looking for flatware.

"Peacocks? Where'd you find peacock eggs?"

"Nowhere. Peacocks don't lay eggs. But peahens do. Was a farm over on the other side of the state, not far from the Green River. Heard women yelling for help," he began, and Susan started, looking up quickly at him. Robert smiled as he continued. "Turned out to be a whole flock of peacocks and peahens. Sound all the world like women screaming for help." He chuckled at the memory, his eyes focused on something three feet beyond the floor. He held two forks in his hand.

"And you went to help?" Susan smiled as she pulled out the pan of crispy bacon.

"You hear someone yelling for help . . ." He looked up at her and shrugged.

"Then you helped yourself to some eggs?" She laid strips of bacon next to the steaming eggs on the plates. Four strips for Robert. A big man needs a big breakfast, her mother always said.

"No, old guy there gave them to me. Had some stories. Old military guy who had found his place in the world as some sort of a developer, but he never stopped being 'The Colonel.'" Robert took his plate from Susan and walked into the dining room. "Nice table," he said, putting his plate on the woven placemat. "New?"

"No, smart ass, just visible finally." Susan laughed and followed him into the dining room.

Chapter 7

Robert tugged on the clothes Susan had bought him yesterday at Wal-Mart. She wouldn't let him go with her, so he couldn't try on anything, but figured surely his former dimensions were pretty much the same. He had objected, at first, when she had suggested she go alone to get him some clothes that would fit better than Johnny's hand-me-downs, or as she had called them, "hand-me-ups," since she considered Robert to be far more the person to admire as well as simply bigger than the mostly absent husband, first, then entirely absent father Johnny had been. But when she had mentioned that everyone would be gawping at Robert's return, he had decided she was right. The time would come soon enough, but perhaps not under the glare of the big box where nearly everyone in town went on Sunday.

It turned out the jean size he recalled was right on the inseam, too large on the waist, but Susan had anticipated that and adjusted her purchase. She told him later finding 30x36-sized pants of any sort wasn't exactly easy. But she had guessed the size correctly. He had lost several inches on his waist, which he had never considered to be exactly pudgy. The stiff denim felt foreign but very welcome – clean, new, solid, something he had not experienced in many years.

She had gotten him only some cotton tee shirts, with the breast pockets he had asked for, in blue and in white. If he had lost weight and inches off his waist, his upper torso was perhaps larger. He certainly wasn't heavier, but his muscles, especially his upper arms, were larger from grappling with rocks and trees to make shelters and deadfall traps, he guessed. She said he looked like a modern-day Tarzan, just swung out of Cooper's Woods rather than darkest Africa. The tees were soft, bright, almost exotic feeling.

He laced up the knock-off canvas tennis shoes. His feet were the same size as ever, fortunately. He wore the final pair of clean white socks his friend he met in the woods many miles from there had given him, although Susan had bought him an eight-pack of new ones. There was something luxurious about so many plush socks at his disposal. He laced the plain brown leather belt through the loops of the jeans. So many new clothes. Where were his old clothes now, since those people had moved into his house? What had they seen fit to do with his things? Bobby's things? He felt his face begin to flush with anger and tried to think of something else.

He tucked in his shirt and stepped out into the hallway from the spare bedroom that was his, but only until he reclaimed his own house. Sure, he was welcome to stay with his sister, and the bed was amazing to sleep on after so long sleeping on pine boughs and piles of leaves and, as often as not, simply the cold hard ground. Besides, she had told him her unemployment was about to run out and he had the resources to help her out, although she had scoffed at the notion. But he could. And he would if she would let him.

He ducked into the bathroom to wash his face and comb his hair. He took a look at himself in the full-length mirror behind the door. He didn't look too bad, he decided. Greyer on top than he expected, but he was fit, still had pretty much the same face, if thinner, same height. He noticed his arms stretched against the sleeves of his shirt.

He looked at his own stern expression in the mirror. He had made up his mind. He was back, back for good. That certitude invigorated him. He could go into town and meet people again and just be himself. Being himself meant still not necessarily telling everyone his business. He had never been one to do that, and now was surely not the time to do that. But Susan told him his old friend Jimmy was still around, although she said he had gotten pretty heavy after hurting himself when Mr. Raney's barn caught fire. He too had been a volunteer fireman. But he was still married to Diana, his college sweetheart he had brought back to live with him on the family farm, growing sorghum and corn.

Robert made up his mind to go visit Jimmy later today, after they went by the lawyer's office. And the bank. What was it about going to the bank that made him a bit anxious? Was it finding out he had a very nice nest egg? He imagined now the look on his pal Jimmy's face when he found Robert on his doorstep and smiled, then blinked, and let a small scowl creep over his cheeks.

He had left Jimmy too, he realized. When he left, he left everyone, and if Susan was accepting and forgiving, she was his sister, and, besides, that was her nature anyway. But what if Jimmy was mad at him? What if Jimmy had mourned Robert's leaving, his passing, as it were, and now would have no room in his heart for an old friend? What if Robert had alienated everyone? He sighed, finished cleaning up, and walked back into the living room. Susan had gotten ready, and Robert thought she looked positively gorgeous. She had on makeup and her hair was done nice, and she even had on a pair of nice slacks and a simple but very pretty muslin blouse. Robert did a double take.

"You got a thing for Martin?"

"What?" Susan was applying lipstick. She gave Robert a wry smile. "No, but I need a job and one never knows."

"Huh," he grunted. "Guess that's why we're going then." She turned and looked at him flatly. He paused, then added, "It's my house. I should just go over and take what is mine back." His voice was angrier than he felt. "That boy can't just take my home."

Susan's mouth dropped. "'That boy?' You went over there, didn't you?" she challenged. "You went over to the house."

"My house," he corrected.

Susan shook her head. "Thought we agreed you'd wait." She headed for the door, picking up her keys from the table en route.

"'Agreed.' It's more like you told me not to. But they didn't see me." He followed, ducking again at the door. "I'm good at that." That felt more like an excuse than anything else.

"Right." Susan shook her head, marching down the sidewalk. "You're not exactly an elf, you know. No one ever notices a man your size outside their window."

"I wasn't outside their window." Was he really apologizing to her for going to his own home? Or just explaining himself. He felt a pique of frustration at the insinuation he was somehow in the wrong here. "I've hidden in the woods for years. If I don't want to be seen, I can manage that quite well." He opened the passenger door and tried to get in the car, but the seat was too far forward from Susan moving it up for her shopping bags. Susan was frozen on the driver's side, watching him with a shocked expression.

"You skulked around in the woods behind the house, *your* house, to spy on them?" she asked incredulously, holding the door open.

"It's my goddamn house," he barked back, angrily fidgeting with the lever to move the seat. He managed to maneuver the seat back with a sudden ratcheting sound. Susan climbed in now and glared at him as he scrunched himself into the little car.

"Don't you curse at me, Robert Younger," she growled. He heard his mother's tone so clearly he had to look over, surprised.

"Yes ma'am," he had to chuckle, and Susan heard what that meant and managed a wan smile herself as she cranked the ignition and started down the street.

Wyler's Ford was a small community, but it was the county seat, so there was always a certain amount of traffic during the day. Inside the car, Robert remained mostly anonymous, but once he unfolded himself from the passenger side in front of the once-storefront-now-office of Martin Douglas, his white-lettered name on the glass door, he saw heads turn. Joe Marks, the mail carrier in his little post office jeep, twisted his head around as he passed, his passenger side driving making Robert very clear. Joe wasn't a bad sort, but anyone on his route through the western half of the county that happened to be out, Joe would have to tell.

And it wasn't a secret, really. Maybe more a matter of privacy. But perhaps if he was the type of magician who could make himself disappear, he could not be surprised at a hubbub when he made himself reappear. He waited for Susan to come around.

Betty Lawson came out from her store next to Martin's offices, her mouth agape. Robert had dated her a couple of times, after Nikki left, but he never felt any chemistry with her. She seemed to like him well enough, and she was attractive and successful in her shop, which was a combination of florist, framing shop, jewelry store, cosmetics counter, and gold buying and selling exchange. But if he and Nikki were long since done after she went away, he was somehow always stuck in a kind of netherworld of what he had once felt and what he feared would happen again.

"Bobby!" Betty yelled and ran towards him. Yes, she had known him since grade school, but he rarely heard that name anymore. That was another thing that had put him off with her when they dated briefly. She knew he preferred "Robert" now, but to her, as well as a few others still around from those childhood days, he would forever be "Bobby." Robert froze. She looked like she wanted to throw herself at him, but he stiffened and stood up straight, so she stopped herself.

"Betty," he said in greeting, with a tone he hoped was warm but not overly so.

Betty stopped a couple of feet away, her arms that had intended to be wrapped around Robert folded up before her. "Why, if you aren't a sight for sore eyes, Bobby," she gushed. Susan shot Robert a look. She knew Bobby was her late nephew's name, not her brother's, but she seemed oddly bemused at his discomfort.

Robert just stood there, feeling very awkward, for a moment. What did he want to say to Betty? Nothing, he realized. Finally, Susan spoke. "How you doing, Betty?" Susan reached out her hand to shake with Betty, who responded with her hand.

"I'm okay, Susan. I'm okay. Been a little rough with the business with the pandemic, but looks like we'll be okay. Know what they say: what doesn't kill you makes you stronger."

"Yeah," Susan said, but Robert saw her make a brief scowl.

"Yeah, Betty," Robert finally managed to say something, even if it was only an echo of his sister. Why was he so tongue-tied? Being around people was maybe going to take some getting used to. "Excuse us, Betty. We've got an appointment." He waved at Martin's door.

"Okay," Betty nodded, as if she were in on a story. Perhaps she was. In a small town like Wyler's Ford, everyone usually was in on whatever the story was. Susan led him through the door and into the law offices. Sherri Marsh, who had been a cheerleader in junior high school with Susan, was sitting behind the desk. Robert remembered her being a pretty little girl, not friends so much as acquaintances with Susan, but she was now heavier, and the years had worn creases into her face. Sherri had them sit in the waiting area, a stark seating space of four leather and chrome chairs with a dusty plastic fern behind them.

When they were seated, Susan looked at him. "That's another one I can't stand," she whispered, a bit too loudly, Robert thought.

"Sherri? I thought you all got along okay." He motioned with his thumb.

"No, Sherri's okay. I hate that whole 'what doesn't kill you makes you stronger' thing. It's just a platitude for long-suffering, which those who cannot find a way out of find oddly reassuring. If it were true that what doesn't kill you makes you stronger, then poverty stricken, starving populations around the globe would be stronger than any other people. That appears to not be the case." Robert grinned at his sister. "What?" She gave him a questioning look.

"You have too much time on your hands, Sis."

Susan sat back into the truly uncomfortable chair and folded her arms defensively. "Huh," she breathed. "Doesn't feel that way to me." Robert sat, watching her, then she looked up and smiled. "I don't know why I've started noticing these things. Just do." She paused. Then she added, "I'd bet you anything Martin is sitting at his desk playing solitaire, making us wait."

"You think?" Then Robert realized he had heard something that made no sense to him. "Wait, pandemic?"

Susan looked over at him, her mouth open in disbelief. "Oh my, you have been a hermit, haven't you?"

"Susan," Martin called across the little waiting area as he came towards them. He was a squat man, a bit on the heavier side than Robert recalled. And losing his hair some. "Robert." Martin stuck his hand out. Robert took his hand, and they shook. It was a solid handshake, Robert decided. Martin did not seem to feel the need to grip as if he had something to prove to Robert, which many men often seemed to do with him, clearly intentionally forcing their grips tighter. "Come on in." He led them to his office where a huge desk sat surrounded by bookshelves. Robert noticed the books were red leather-bound with gold lettering. He paused to look at the array. "Something, huh?" Martin was sitting in his swivel chair behind his desk. "They were my daddy's. Complete set of Kentucky Revised Statutes through 1965." He turned to look at them himself. "Gave them to me when he retired from the bench." He swiveled back to face them, grinning. "Almost never use them," he chuckled. "Too much easier to use this." He patted the laptop sitting to one side of the blotter on his desk. He turned to admire the books again. "But they do make a great backdrop for video calls." He turned back around grinning, and finally Robert sat next to where Susan already was seated in the vinyl and chrome chair identical to the ones in the waiting area. "So," Martin leaned forward, suddenly serious, "Susan tells me you've got someone living in your house." He left the sentence hanging, as if it were a question. Robert nodded.

69

"They're squatters. I looked it up," Susan chimed in. "I think it's called 'derelict property.'" That sounded to Robert like both a question and an attempt at making an impression on Martin. She really was trying to get a job offer.

"Well, no." Martin shook his head. "It's really more like adverse possession." There was a pause.

"What's that?" Robert and Susan asked together.

"Adverse possession is a legal principle through which squatters try to get legal custody of a property if the true owner doesn't object within a certain amount of time."

"I do object," Robert felt his insides tighten with anger. "Someone can just take my property? That doesn't make any sense."

"No," Martin held up his hand in a stop motion. "No, they can't, and they don't have any legal ground to claim your house."

"So they're trespassing," Susan offered.

"Well, no. Not really. At least, not in legal terms. Trespassing is a criminal matter, but squatting is something for civil court."

"If I, we, take back my house and they don't go, are they trespassing then?" Robert scowled.

"Um, yes, in that case, I think they would be."

"Martin," Robert leaned forward. "It's my house. Can't I just go over there and throw them out? I don't get it. Where are my rights as the owner?"

"You mean, as in physically pick them up and carry them out?" Martin raised his eyebrows. "I think that would be unwise."

"But, they're trespassers," he paused, "and thieves." Robert moved farther forward, feeling himself growing agitated. "If you came home and found burglars in your home, wouldn't you be right in chasing them out?" He raised his eyebrows, his frustration growing.

"They're not thieves, are they?" Martin leaned back in his Naugahyde swivel chair and placed his fingertips together thoughtfully.

"Sure," Robert felt his voice raise and he tried to calm himself with a moment of breathing, then continued. "Look, I had stuff in my house. Not a lot, but it was mine." He swallowed. "Mine and . . ." He felt his throat tighten.

"And Bobby's," Susan finished. Robert glanced over, grateful for the help.

"Ah," Martin put his hands on his desk blotter and leaned forward. "I see. Well, we don't know that any of that is missing as yet, do we?" Robert looked back, somehow feeling vaguely hopeful. Maybe the things were still there, somewhere. He leaned back onto the chair now. As if his posture answered Martin's question, Martin continued. "Let's look at the big picture first, then focus on where your situation comes in, shall we?" Robert nodded.

"Yes, please go ahead, Martin." Susan again found words for Robert, who was still feeling new to this whole return-to-talking-with-people thing.

"Okay, so in Kentucky, someone is a squatter who takes occupancy of an unoccupied building, or even a piece of land that has been abandoned. They explicitly do so, knowingly, without permission. Now, squatting is actually legal and fairly common. The issue is when they want to claim adverse possession." Martin talked and Robert listened. "Now, here in the USA, squatters have five things they have to do to claim legal adverse possession to the place." Martin began enumerating on his fingers.

"First, they have to stay on the property for an uninterrupted stretch of time. But here's the very good news: in Kentucky, that time period is fifteen years." Robert felt his stomach muscles loosen. "Now I think Terry and Charlene meet the other four requirements, but that doesn't matter."

Robert looked up sharply, but Susan again anticipated his words. "You know these people, Martin?" she asked.

"No," Martin held up his hands in a surrender motion. "But you asked me to look into it, Susan, so I did."

Robert glanced over at Susan, grateful. Then he managed to find some words. "So, what other things are they doing that meet the requirements?"

Martin looked relieved to be able to continue. "Well, they

have to live there, just their family, not some sort of commune."
He counted again on his fingers.

"Like a bunch of druggies?" Susan offered and shot Robert a glance.

"Yeah," Martin answered. "Yeah, like a bunch of druggies. Also," he pressed a third finger, "they aren't trying to hide the fact they are there." He pressed a fourth finger. "They are obviously living there and treating it as if they owned it. And finally, although this one I don't know if they have everything right on, but we can find out, they seem to recognize that their squatting is what they call 'hostile.'"

"Hostile?" Susan asked.

"I can be hostile," Robert muttered, a bit louder than he meant to.

"That is a legal term, Robert, not an emotional one." Martin continued. Robert felt a little admonished and didn't especially like the feeling. "It just means, they don't know you, they know they don't actually own it, and that they are acting in good faith. This one is maybe another place they fail to meet the requirements for claiming ownership. They would have to think they had a deed or a color of title claim, but even if they did, that requirement would only take it down to seven years of living there, and if my research is correct, they've been there about five, Robert." Robert digested this. These people had lived in his house for five years? "So, here's what I propose," Martin continued. "And this first part is critical, Robert." Robert looked up. "We have to keep it civil with the Jeters." Robert mulled the name. It wasn't familiar. "Being civil and calm and even respectful, Robert, might help convince them not to do any damage to the place, and you sure don't want that, and might actually help convince them to move out without having to evict them, which can be more time consuming and often makes everyone unhappy. I will notify them in writing that they need to move out of the house, and I will give them a deadline. That way, they can have a little time to find another place."

"I really just want them out." Robert was bristling a bit

at the notion he needed reminding to be civil. Did he have a reputation as a hothead? Maybe he had been, before, but not anymore. Then again, who knew this new Robert, this Robert who had spent six years in the back country, communing with nature, communing with himself?

"Robert, if we use some empathy, maybe even help them find another place to live, I promise you it will go better." Martin was looking over his glasses at Robert.

"Okay, okay. I get it." Robert took a breath. "But I can't even go over there and check on my house?"

"I wouldn't go in, no. Let me work through the process. You can always go on your land, but don't create a confrontation. It won't look good and will probably just make them more stubborn."

"Okay, we will do it your way." Robert nodded. He closed his mouth tight so he wouldn't say, "For now."

Susan and Robert left the office, and Robert squeezed himself into the car again. "Think you could drop me off at Jimmy's?" He looked over at his sister. He recalled that Jimmy had had a bit of a crush on Susan back in school, although he had never told her so, deferring to his friendship with Robert.

"Yeah, sure." She turned on the car and put it in gear. "But first, you need to go by the bank." Then she shot him a grin. "You're going to enjoy that." She backed out of the parking space and headed down the street.

Chapter 8

Luke slipped out the back door while Rosie was watching her favorite cartoon show, "The Gentle Bears." It wasn't that he disliked Rosie, but he sometimes felt like he never had any time just to himself. She might have been alerted to the fact he was going to get away by the fact he allowed her to watch the show about the stupid bears rather than the ninja cartoon he always liked, but she was so happy to get her way, she never suspected a thing.

But Luke needed some alone time, some boy time. It was bad enough they shared a bedroom, her twin bed nearly touching his. They watched television together, played on the long porch with his small metal cars and trucks at the same time, swung on the tire swing together. Any place he wanted to go, she wanted to go too. Most days, she was as attached to him as sap to the bark of a tree. He just wanted a little time by himself.

That was especially true today because he had a new toy to play with. No, it wasn't a toy. Toys are for babies, and Luke was no baby, at least not anymore. This was a tool, a knife. It was, in fact, a real, actual, folding pocketknife with a blade that folded out on each end, one long and tapered, the other shorter and more rounded. He had traded with his school friend JJ for it. JJ had found it in a box in his Grandpa's garage and brought it to school where every boy had lusted after it. It was so cool. Every one of their friends had wanted it, but Luke was JJ's best friend, and he had agreed to trade Luke's baseball glove for it. Sure, the knife had some rust on it, and the longer blade was hard to get out, but it was worth it. Now Luke had his own pocketknife, just like his daddy.

Luke guided the screen door shut so it wouldn't slam and alert Rosie or their dad, who was still asleep after working the late shift at the prison. Mom had already gone to her job at the daycare. Luke wished she would take Rosie along sometime, just so he could have some free time, but she said Rosie was too old for the center. From Luke's perspective, Rosie was not really too old for much. She was such a baby, not like Luke, who was already moving up to the third grade next year, while Rosie was only now finishing up kindergarten.

He stepped off the porch and went behind the tool shed to his secret hiding place, where he kept his most prized possessions. If the things he kept there weren't supposed to be found by his parents especially did not mean he was doing something wrong, exactly. It was just that these were his private things.

He moved the loose plank behind the building and pulled out the small green dented metal box with the hinged top that had at one time held notecards. It was a perfect box for him. He couldn't believe his luck when he found it in the trash behind the dentist's office. He sat in the soft dirt against the back of the shed and opened the box.

There were some marbles he had found at the playground in the town center and the round cardboard cylinder that still had a dozen or so bbs in it. He reached past the thirty-seven cents he had gathered from various spottings of coins along sidewalks, a skill he felt particularly gifted at. The cellophane-wrapped piece of hard candy no longer looked quite edible, but he still kept it, just in case. He never knew when he might need it. There was the knife. The brown plastic handle had grooves molded into it, so it looked a bit like wood. He held the knife in one hand, took out a rubber band from the box, replaced the other treasures, and turned around to shove it behind the board again.

"Lukie?" It was Rosie, calling from the porch. He hated

being called "Lukie." That was a baby's name. He was Luke. Luke Jeter. He flattened himself against the back of the wooden building, hiding, but she couldn't see through wood, or the various tools stored within the building, so his stealth was wasted. "Lukie? Where are you?"

He wished she would stop. She was going to wake up Dad, and then he might come looking for him. He needed a little time. He had a big project in mind with his new knife. He heard the screen door slam shut. He winced. *Keep it up*, he thought. *You'll wake up Dad and then I'm going to be in big trouble.* He was pretty sure his parents didn't want him to have a knife, and, in truth, he knew JJ had stolen it, more or less, from his Grandpa's house. But if his Grandpa wasn't using it, was it really stealing? Luke decided maybe not.

Luke stood and shoved the knife into the right front pocket of his cutoff shorts and stretched around his fingers the thick rubber band from a mess of broccoli his mother had cooked up. It was almost worth eating broccoli in order to get the rubber band. Almost.

Then he slinked into the woods. He loved the weight of the knife in his pocket. He felt grown because of it. He twirled the rubber band between his two index fingers, turning his hands around and around, stretching the elastic, feeling its resistance. All he needed was a good-sized stick that forked. It had to be strong enough for the rubber band to tie to it, and long enough on each branch for a rock to pass through.

Luke was almost hopping with excitement. He had a knife, and soon he would have a slingshot. He was going to be able to go hunting, just like Daddy, although Daddy used the old shotgun Granddad gave him back when he was a teenager. Perhaps he could even go with his daddy on one of his hunts. They could both bring back a squirrel, or maybe even a rabbit. He had wanted a slingshot ever since Frankie's brother got one from the Ace store in town. They spent the afternoon taking turns trying to hit steel cans with pieces of crushed limestone from the alleyway behind Frankie's house. It was true Luke never hit a can, nor even got close, but he was certain that was simply a matter of practice, and once he had his own, he would become a great shooter.

Luke followed one of the several trails that seemed to meander through the woods, often ending in the underbrush without notice. His daddy said they were Indian trails, but the way his father looked at him when he said it, his eyes bugging out as if it were a scary story or something, he knew he was kidding. Besides, Luke wasn't afraid of Indians. They had studied them in school, about how they had helped the first settlers. Luke had even made a diorama about it using plastic cowboy and Indian figures taped to the inside of a battered shoe box. Still, he kept listening for them as he walked through the woods. A part of him wondered if, even now, some brave was spying on him. It couldn't hurt to be careful.

Once Luke felt he was far enough away from the house not to be seen by Rosie, and maybe his daddy, he started scouring the forest floor for the right stick. He kicked at the ground, dislodging small stones and twigs, but nothing that looked like slingshot material. Finally, he picked up one thicker piece, but when he tested the forks, one of them broke right off, clearly rotted through. But he would keep looking. This was too important to give up.

He walked deeper into the woods. He went through a few more stumpy branches before he decided he needed to just cut the piece he needed from a little tree somewhere. He had a knife, after all. That's what it was for. And that way, it wouldn't be rotten.

He climbed across a huge fallen tree and up a long, steep hillside, where he found a stand of saplings growing in the newfound sunlight that resulted from the tree fall. One little tree had a place where it divided almost evenly between two smaller limbs about four feet up, and each side looked pretty strong.

Luke shoved the rubber band into his left pocket and dug out the pocketknife from his right one. He had to stop for just a moment and admire the knife. It was beautiful. He stuck his thumbnail into the tiny groove in the blade and tugged at it. It was stubborn, but he finally got it open, although he did tear his nail a little. Open, the knife was even more impressive. Luke held it in his hand and swished it back and forth several times, as if he were fighting bad guys, even scary Indians. Then he set to work cutting on the small tree.

It was slow going. Luke had believed the knife would whisk through the little tree trunk like dipping into a jar of jelly with a table knife, but the blade was not all that sharp, and the very green wood was tougher than he expected. But he kept at it, sawing at the wood, then going around and around the tree, cutting and hoping at some point the cuts would meet.

This was harder work than he thought it would be. He kept cutting for a long time. Finally, he felt he had cut it pretty much through, so he bent the tree over, and the little tree split, and even where he had cut, the wood was full of wiry, wet shards of wood. This was far more than he had counted on.

But the branched part was still together, so he decided he only needed to pull down the half of the spindly trunk to where he could saw the wood against a rock, maybe. He tugged the tree over, the sapling splitting all the way down. Then he held the green tree down and sawed on the bottom of his slingshot handle, using a log lying on the ground beneath as his cutting board.

The cutting was a bit easier this way, but his arm was getting tired by the time he finally removed the stalk from the two branches. The split trunk sprung up slowly to where it had been, except it was now split and ruined-looking. He sat down on the ground and held up his work.

The two tiny limbs still sported twigs and small leaves. He had spent a lot of energy, but he had made progress. Now he needed to cut the branched parts off. That had to be easier, he decided. They were smaller. He wondered if any braves sneaking around in the woods had anything as wonderful as a slingshot.

Luke tried to chop the smaller branches off by holding the branches on the log and pressing down as hard as he could, but the cutting was still slow. He turned the wood over and cut on the other side, then back on the first side. He did this over and over, until he finally had his handle free from its straggling sprouts. He held it up. It was a pretty good "Y," he decided.

This was going to be so great. He bet even his daddy would think it was cool, although there was the matter of the knife to explain, and that he was pretty sure he wasn't allowed to actually have a slingshot.

Luke gripped the slingshot and aimed as if he had a rubber band on it already. He even pulled back on an imaginary band as if he were going to shoot a rock into the air. There was a knot on one side of the handle that bit into either his palm or his middle finger, depending on which way he held it.

No problem, he decided. He would simply whittle the rough place out and make it smooth with his new, wonderful, folding knife. He was seated on the log now, the one he had used for his cutting board. He tried to whittle the knot out of the stick, but the blade kept sticking on the gnarled wood, so he put the slingshot on his leg to give him a better angle and some resistance. The Y of the handle straddled his left leg, and he placed the knife along the edge of the stick to push through the edge of the tough barb of wood.

A huge hand suddenly covered his hand that held the knife poised to push down towards his lap. Luke caught his breath and opened his eyes wide, but he did not look up. It had to be the Indian brave, come to get him for certain. His Daddy had not been kidding after all.

Luke felt his heart pounding against his ribs. He heard a faint "Eeerrr" of fear come out of his mouth that he didn't intend to vocalize. He wanted to look up, but knew that looking up meant seeing a terrifying Indian ghost or something, something he could not explain, exactly, but something terrible. His legs trembled.

"Don't do that," a man said in a deep scratchy voice.

Now Luke had to look at whoever it was. He looked up, and it didn't seem to be an Indian but a very tall man whose arm seemed to reach from the sky. Or maybe he was an Indian and now they wore blue jeans and white tee shirts. His huge hand was still on Luke's.

"What?" Luke's voice was faint, quaky. "Do what?" For just a moment, he decided maybe it was JJ's Grandpa and Luke had been caught with the stolen knife. But he didn't look like a Grandpa, exactly.

The man looked down at him without frowning or smiling, just looking at him. Then he said, "Don't ever pull a knife towards your body. You're about to put a gash in your leg, boy."

"What?" Luke felt a tightness in his throat. He wanted to call for his daddy, but that moment wasn't really sure just which direction to call. He in fact had no idea at that instant which way the house was.

"Look at where your knife is pointing." The man let go of his hand and stood up straight. From where Luke was sitting, it looked like he was as tall as the trees. Luke stared up, frozen. "Look," the man said again, motioning with his hand. Luke looked back at his slingshot; the knife poised just above his thigh. Okay, he saw what the man was saying. "If your blade slips, you've got a cut in your leg in a very, very bad place. Cut yourself there, you maybe don't make it out of the woods." Luke looked up at the man again. Luke couldn't find any words. The man shook his head. "Always push the blade away from your body so you don't cut yourself."

"Okay?" Luke looked up again, his answer more question than affirmation. He felt a very strong urge to pee right where he was. The man stood there, staring down at him, as if trying to figure out something. He didn't speak for what seemed like a very long time, but it probably wasn't. He just stared down at Luke.

Finally, the man blinked a slow blink and squatted down beside him, although he was still much taller than Luke. "Making a slingshot?" His voice was softer now, still coarse but more like a man than the ghost of an Indian brave.

"Yes, sir." If Luke could have figured out how to run away,

he would, but in truth, he had no clue which way was home.

The man reached down and took the whittled stick from his hand. Luke did not resist. "You don't need to cut off the knot. Wrap it with some maple bark from that poor tree you mangled." The man nodded towards the split sapling Luke had cut on. "Look." The man stood again, his head towering in the leaves.

He stepped over to the little tree and pulled a fixed-bladed knife from a leather sheath along his belt. He dropped the slingshot to the ground and kneeled over the tree. He cut two long lines in the small trunk with the point of the knife. Then he used the sharp edge of the blade and his thumb to scrape a corner of bark free, until he could grab it with a finger and his thumb. He ripped it off slowly in a single long strand.

Luke watched him working. The man picked up the slingshot and wrapped the handle, covering the knot. He tucked the end of the strip into a place where the bark had circled around the stick, then pulled it gently until it was pressed around the wood. "See?" He bent over and handed the slingshot back to Luke. Luke took it and gripped it. The knot didn't bite into his hand at all and, what was more, the slingshot looked even cooler with the wrapping. Luke looked up. He was trying to figure out who this guy was. "Where's your band?" the man said. At first, Luke wasn't sure what he meant and simply looked up at him. "You have a piece of rubber or something?" The man's eyebrows raised.

"Oh, yeah." Luke managed to stand now. He fished in his pocket and brought out the rubber band. He handed it to the man. The man raised one eyebrow doubtfully, then looked back at Luke. He reached out and Luke put the wrapped slingshot in his great big hand. The man cut the rubber band in two, then tied one end to each side of the slingshot. He tested the pull a couple of times, then handed it back to Luke.

"You need a little pouch of some sort to hold the rock, but this will work on a very small stone."

"Okay," Luke looked down at the slingshot. It was perfect.

He looked up at the man who turned and walked several feet away. "Thanks, Mister."

The man stopped and turned and looked down at Luke. There was almost something like a smile on his face, but then his face seemed angry again. "Don't shoot the birds. You hear me?"

Luke gulped and stepped back. "Yes, sir."

"These are my birds, you got that?"

"Yes, sir." Luke felt himself tremble again.

The man turned halfway around. "Go home," he growled, scowling at Luke. Luke looked around himself. He would go home, if he only knew how. The man raised his arm and pointed down the hill opposite where the fallen tree was. "That way."

The man blinked and stepped back into the woods. Luke followed him with his eyes for a few minutes. The man didn't make a sound in the woods. Luke started down the hill in the direction the man had pointed. He debated what to say to his daddy. He had a slingshot and a knife, neither of which he was supposed to have. The story of the giant man in the forest was one he ached to tell, but maybe not just yet.

It turned out he was not nearly as far from his house as he had imagined. He replaced the knife in the file box and slid the slingshot next to the box behind the board. He went into the kitchen where Rosie was eating a toasted frozen waffle and his daddy was drinking a cup of coffee, hunched over a cell phone.

"You hungry?" his daddy asked, but Luke was already putting a waffle in the toaster.

Chapter 9

Robert strode up the long dirt and river gravel road. If some things had changed over the years, this road had not. Susan had offered him a ride to Jimmy's house, but the truth was, her car was such a tight fit for him, the walk of several miles was far more comfortable than riding. And he was used to walking. Besides, he wanted to take a short cut past his own house, and she would not have approved of that, and, frankly, Robert was in no mood for a lecture. Granted, it actually was not a shorter route to walk back by his old spread at the edge of Cooper's Woods on the way to Jimmy's. In fact, it was at least a half mile out of the way, but he wanted to check on things. And the way he saw it, it was his house, after all. Everyone agreed with that, or at least, everyone who mattered to Robert.

It was still his house and his property. Susan nor anyone else should be able to keep him from going to his own place and checking on things. It was true Martin had convinced him to be patient, that Martin could handle it in an appropriate fashion, a less confrontational one, although patience had never been Robert's nature in the past. But living off the land had at least taught him that, and more. So, Robert decided to just hike past the house and maybe stop for a few minutes to scope out his little homestead from the stand of trees that grew on the rise behind the place.

There was a slight breeze blowing across the hilltop. The

new purple leaves of the sumac tree caught his eye, as it always had. Robert surveyed the place, so familiar to him, but also strange, in its way, with a different family living there, a pink pony riding toy on its side behind the porch. But the yard was mowed and overall, it looked tidy. And he had to admit, the garden beside the house looked pretty good. He himself had spent years enriching the soil in the very spot the garden now grew in. But that was a long time ago. No, these newcomers had done most of this now, these squatters, who presumed to take over his house and his land simply because they wanted to.

He stood beside a path now, having left the road just before reaching his little house. He was mostly hidden by an eastern pine, but no one seemed to be around. Then he remembered he himself had planted this pine, he and his son. It had been their Christmas tree so many years before. Now it was tall, and the needles that provided him a hidden vantage point reached down from branches growing farther up rather than from below.

Bobby had been little, maybe eight. They had planted the tree together and now, it was very tall. Robert reached up and touched the scaly bark that held the wispy needles. Around him, cones were scattered around the brown refuse of spikes. He had made so many beds from just such a find of fallen pine straw on his travels. Bobby had loved watching the tree grow, and towards the end, maybe the Christmas before he went off to war, had decorated the tree himself with popcorn and apples for the animals to enjoy. Robert felt a smile spread across his cheeks at the memory.

This was an unexpected recollection, a happy one, he and Bobby sitting in their flannel coats as still as possible on the long back porch while deer and squirrels munched away on the found treats. Even now, he remembered the gleam in Bobby's eyes as he watched the creatures enjoying his little gift. He was all grown by then, but he could not hide his boyish glee at the animals appreciating, in their innocent animal way, his beneficence.

Robert peered around the tree towards the porch where they had sat. There it was, and there still was his own rocking chair that he had inherited from a great aunt, a massive oak chair left to him by his own massive oak of an aunt who had scolded him and spoiled him, in turn, whenever he had visited with Susan, Daryl, Poppa, and Momma, so very long ago. His roots were so very deep here. There was the pine tree he stood beneath, of course, the cabin he had mostly built himself, the family history, the memories. He had taken all those memories for granted before, when he had left. No, even worse, he had spurned them, as if the memories were the reason for his sorrow.

No matter now. Now, he knew better. Now, he would relish every last one of them and even make new ones. Once he got these people out of his house, he and Susan would have holidays here. He would get out all the old music, if it was still around. These people had probably had a yard sale and sold everything just to get rid of it.

The thought of music brought him back. He pulled a flute from his back pocket then stooped under the low hanging branches and sat, leaning up against the scruffy trunk. He started playing. He started with the tunes he had taught himself over the years, not anything anyone would know, just melodies he had managed to pick out that he liked the sound of. If some of them sounded like songs he remembered from before, he couldn't exactly say, but he was okay with that too. Then he thought that since he had had the holiday memory, he might try to play a song he recalled from the albums he and Bobby used to listen to on his old phonograph.

True Value. He could see the wooden elves on the evergreen on the cover. Papa had passed it along. "We Three Kings" would be a good one, he decided, as Henry Mancini might have played it if he had a homemade recorder made from bamboo. It didn't take long; it's a simple tune, given to a haunting melody. Once he had played it through, he put down the recorder and sat there for a few minutes. It was a new beginning. Yes, Robert could do this.

The scent of the pine and the Christmas memory blended into a kind of glow within him. It was early May now, and the holidays were far away, but that was something Nikki had shared with him before she left; embracing the music and movies of the Christmas season pretty much year around. How strange it might sound, he thought, to hear a reedy version of "We Three Kings" played in the woods in springtime. But if he wanted to play a song, who would say he could not, he thought.

He climbed out from under the tree and shoved the recorder into his back pocket again. He still needed practice on the song, but there was time – lots of time. He ambled down the incline and walked along the garden plot. There were onion sets and tomato plants along one row. Pepper plants lined another furrow, and other long mounds of dirt looked to be planted with seeds of some sort. It looked like there were hills for corn and green beans. It was a traditional layout. He could tell they had some experience with gardening. He liked the garden they had planted. If his appreciation was begrudging, it was there, nonetheless.

He watched for movement around the house, but the car was gone, and no one seemed to be around. Goldfinches, still sporting their drabber winter coats, flitted from a feeder near the back porch. A whirl-a-gig on a skinny wooden staff twirled in the flowerbed by the side yard where the sharp green leaves of irises jabbed up through the soil. He and Nikki had planted those, heirlooms from someone's grandparents' house, somewhere, but Robert couldn't say just whose. But they were familiar, just the same.

Robert decided to take a closer look at the vegetable patch. It was where he had made his garden, back before he had left. It was rich soil with good drainage. Robert had added compost and fertilizer every year. Before. He wondered if this couple was being as diligent. The garden looked good. He walked along the edge and checked out the plants. The potatoes had been planted early, so that was good. They actually looked almost ready to bloom. There would be new potatoes available in only a few weeks. He walked along the tomato sets. A few needed suckering, so he stooped down and pinched off the water growth as he went, throwing the small green segments towards the woods.

Return of the Goatman

He heard a car approaching, so he stepped quickly behind the house, then slipped behind the little wood storage building. The sedan puttered up the road, then came to a stop in front of the house. Now Robert felt awkward. If he had every right to be at his own property, why was he hiding? He was acting as if stepping on his own land was somehow against the rules. He should just walk out and greet whoever had driven up and, in fact, tell them to get the hell out of his house. "Hello!" he could say. "What are you doing on my property? You need to get lost."

He could feel the anger in him rising. And by the way, where were his possessions, he would ask. No doubt they had either kept them, or maybe even sold them for far too little for a bit of cash. It wasn't their compound bow, he figured; they likely sold it for a song. And the record player and the vinyl records were likely gone too. If they considered the house abandoned, then maybe all his belongings were so much trash to be discarded. He heard car doors slam shut, the echo-y sound of a small car made inexpensively. Robert's truck didn't sound like that. It was solid. Susan told him Jimmy had it in his barn. It was as if everyone had circled his belongings like vultures once he left.

He felt his face flush. He needed to try to calm down. If he went in and got into an altercation with this Jeter fellow, it would only make things worse. Martin had emphasized that. Robert wasn't afraid of much of anything, but he knew getting in a fight so soon after coming back would convince pretty much everyone he was somehow in the wrong.

Robert decided now was not the right time. He had not let anything have a chance yet to work. Martin would not have even had time to get his letter out. Robert turned around and pressed his back against the wood of the shed. A board knocked loose from the bottom, but he did not stop to replace it. He heard the children in the yard and knew he had a narrow window to walk away.

He stepped quickly, straight back into the woods, keeping the shed between himself and the house. He had learned through the years how little people saw of what they did not expect to see, although children, of course, seemed to see everything. Once he had reached the rise where the poplars and shagbark hickories grew thick, he let himself relax and simply slip around the hill and out of sight.

Walking along a game path now, familiar because of the rise of hills and fall of narrow valleys rather than the vegetation that had changed so dramatically in the past six years, he let himself feel a calm come over him. He heard a plaintive child's cry behind him, on the other side of the hill, and another in some sort of response, but he ignored them. Now he was simply a man walking through the woods like so many others in these parts. Morels were up. Lots of people were in the woods, so his presence there shouldn't mean anything.

He pulled out the recorder and played through the Christmas song again. He found the tricky note he had missed before and reminded himself how he found it now as he stepped through the forest. The children's voices grew quiet. He realized that while it might not be odd to be traipsing through the forest, ambling along playing Christmas songs was perhaps unusual. He slid the little recorder into his back pocket and climbed up the hill.

By the time he made Jimmy's house, he had worked up a thirst and felt his stomach rumble. Eating so much at Susan's had created a larger appetite in him. He glanced around at what might be available along the crushed limestone driveway. There were dandelions coming up he could munch on, if he could find a bit of water to rinse off the dust from the rock. There were plenty of wild violets, and plantain was up. But he resisted the urge to start chomping on the weeds in Jimmy's yard.

People already thought he was half off his roller skate. If he started grazing in people's yards, it just wouldn't look good. Maybe he could practice his moo-ing, and then he would blend right in. No, he would make do for now. Jimmy knew he was coming, and no doubt Diana would have some cookies or something. Cookies would be okay. Truth was, Robert had never had much of a sweet tooth, but upon his return, he had discovered he now had one. Perhaps all those years without sugar had done it. Robert's mouth watered. Yes, a peanut butter scotch cookie like Susan had made last night would be welcome. He heard the growling of a tractor heading his way and soon he saw Jimmy, bouncing atop the old red Farmall, heading in his direction. Robert saw Jimmy's familiar blue and white cap first, although the bill was thread-bare, and there was a visible sweat stain around the band. Jimmy was grinning.

"Robert!" Jimmy waved with his left hand, his right hand still pushing the throttle. Robert worried the tractor might veer out of control, but it was chugging along slowly enough, it would likely make no difference. Jimmy returned his hand to the wheel and throttled back, and the tractor lurched forward slowly, then stopped, the engine dying. Jimmy jumped off the seat and stomped his muddy feet towards Robert. "Robert Younger, damnations, man. If you ain't a sight." He reached his massive arms around Robert's shoulders and hugged him. He was bigger around, as Susan had warned him, but he was still strong. He tightened his grip on Robert's shoulders then lifted, taking Robert to his tiptoes. It had always been his greeting to Robert, since they were boys, Robert being the taller but Jimmy always stouter.

"Let me down, Jimmy," Robert called in mock anguish. Jimmy lowered him, then clapped Robert on the back.

"Robert," Jimmy said again, as if saying it confirmed his old friend was back home. He stood back and Robert was sure he saw a glistening in Jimmy's eyes. Jimmy was a bear of a man, had always been, but in truth, he could tear up about almost anything sentimental.

If coming home had been an unknown adventure for Robert, being back with Jimmy was not. It was as if Robert had just come back from fishing for smallies in one of the streams on the ridge and Jimmy was just glad to have him home in time for the softball tournament. Robert felt a tinge of guilt for having taken his friendship so much for granted. He made himself a quiet promise not to do so again.

Jimmy set his mouth, looking as if he were determined not to show just how emotional he felt. He turned and climbed back on the old tractor in a familiar three step dance, pulled out the throttle, and pushed the starter button. He turned his head around and shouted over the rumble of the engine, "Climb on, Robert." He motioned with the bill of his cap at the drawbar behind his seat.

The old tractor still ran. It had always been Jimmy's talent: keeping things running. He had learned it from his father and cultivated it through high school. Robert had a sudden recollection of the 1970 Super Bee Jimmy had spent every cent and every waking moment redoing when they were teens. If Robert was the carpenter, Jimmy was the mechanic. Jimmy could fix anything, and did, whether it was gasoline, diesel, or even electrical. He could just take it apart and figure out why it wasn't working and fix it.

Robert stepped up on the hitch and leaned forward, holding onto Jimmy's shoulders as they took a wide turn and headed back over the hill. It occurred to Robert to ask about the old Dodge, if Jimmy still tinkered with it, or if he had sold it. He remembered Jimmy turning down large offers at the annual Founder's Day Parade in Wyler's Ford, the old cars being an annual entrant. But the tractor was too loud to try to talk over.

He watched over Jimmy's bouncing head, through the vaguely blue exhaust pumping through the pipe on the engine. He saw Jimmy and Diana's little spread open up before him. The Barlow Farm. Jimmy's family had been on the place for at least four generations, and even though Jimmy had loved going off to school, there was never any doubt in Robert's mind he would come back. There was the white house with its lap siding, looking solid, if perhaps ready for a fresh coat of paint. But it was still springtime. Painting could wait a bit. The sycamore tree that had stood in the center of the dusty circle of a drive was still there. Jimmy's great grandmother had planted it over a buried hound dog, was the story that had come down through the years. Jimmy's Dad always joked it was a dogwood tree as a result. There was a gathering of brightly painted metal shell-back chairs beneath the tree, along with a fire pit and a long log for sitting on.

Diana was spreading a cloth over a small table. She looked the same. She too was perhaps a bit heavier than before, but she had always been pretty, and back when Jimmy and Robert used to sit by this very fire pit, drinking canned beer, Jimmy had often grown contemplative talking about her, how lucky he felt to have found a girl that wanted to be with him, and, to Jimmy, she was the very prettiest one.

Diana heard the tractor and looked up. She waved, and Robert took a hand off Jimmy's back to wave back. As if on cue, the tractor lurched, and Robert had to reach back quickly to keep his balance.

The door of the house opened, and a sturdy young woman came out carrying a bowl covered with plastic wrap between her hands. She wore jeans and a royal blue sweatshirt. It took just a moment for Robert to recognize her as Carla, Jimmy and Diana's daughter. She was grown. If Robert had been asked to describe Carla Barlow, he would have pictured the gangly teenager who had as obvious a crush on Bobby as a girl could have, although Bobby had always thought of her more as a little sister than any sort of romantic interest. But here she was, walking towards the table now, her face beaming a smile towards Robert. She looked just like her mother, dark haired, short, but even walking to the table with the bowl, she seemed to have an air of confidence now she had lacked as a teen. Diana had teased her when she was younger about Bobby, how the two of them made such a pretty couple. Robert watched her place the bowl on the table, then come running towards the tractor, which Jimmy stopped several yards away from the seating area.

Robert stepped off the tractor and Carla threw her arms around his waist. "Uncle Robert," she said, grinning, looking up at him. "You're home."

Robert swallowed the lump in his throat. "I am." He wrapped his long arms around her and gave her a hug. She had called him her uncle since she was able to talk, a term of endearment he had never tired of. Diana came over and gave Robert a sidelong hug, since Carla had not let go of Robert's waist yet.

"Welcome home, Robert," Diana said with a smile, but there was something held back in her greeting. Robert blinked a few times. He knew what it was. If Jimmy and Carla were so very happy to see Robert, Diana no doubt recalled her family's worry over him, their sorrow at his leaving. She would be okay, Robert knew, but she might take a while to completely forget what Robert had put his best friend through.

"Thank you." Robert wanted to apologize for having left, for what he had put them through, for all of it, but right now didn't seem like the right moment. It would come. He just needed to wait. Diana watched him as he mulled this over, and he couldn't escape the feeling that she was reading his thoughts. He hoped so.

Finally, Diana turned and walked back towards the house. She called over her shoulder, "Let go of Robert, Carla. Come get the sandwiches with me." Carla let go, looked up at Robert again with a grin, then trotted off after her mother. The thought of sandwiches was a pleasant one for Robert.

"Hey, Robert, come up to the barn." Jimmy walked up next to him. "I gotta show you something." Jimmy tromped off towards the barn and Robert moved quickly to walk with him. He figured Jimmy had the Bee up and running. He looked forward to taking a spin in it. He looked forward to a lot of things, he realized.

Chapter 10

Jimmy swung the sagging wooden barn door open, its damaged corner dragging along an already worn rut that carved an arc in the dirt. Jimmy lifted the door to finish opening it. The door leaned heavily on its hinges towards the wall of the building.

Robert walked into the space and blinked, letting his eyes adjust to the stark contrast of dark and light. The barn was cool and smelled of hay and gasoline and oil. Streaks of light came between the boards, and particles of amber dust floated upward in the light. There was straw along the edge of the open area, but where Robert expected to see the green-go painted Dodge was his own old Ford pickup truck, although it looked brand new, or at least, shiny and clean.

It had been a burgundy color when he bought it, but the paint had faded to the point that Jimmy and Daryl both teased him he drove a pink pickup. But now, it looked burgundy again, almost. It wasn't repainted, just washed and coated with a deep cleaning wax and thoroughly buffed. It looked great to Robert. The truck had once been one of his most important belongings. It was his office where he kept plans for the buildings he had contracted to work on. It was his workbench at times. He carried lumber and tools everywhere in it. And when he had wanted to go off with his son or his friends, it was how they got there.

"Wow." He walked over to the bed of the truck. Even

that was clean and waxed, although a few scratches in the bed remained. He could even remember what caused some of the scrapes: a propane tank he took to a house he was putting gas logs in that slid the length of the bed and dented the front of the bed when he backed up the hill; nails in the old barn he and Jimmy and Bobby had salvaged lumber from to build the storage building behind his little house. He ran his hand along the edge of the truck bed. He turned and looked at Jimmy, who was watching him from the doorway.

"She's as good as new, Robert, and as far as I know, she's still yours."

All Robert could see was the silhouette of his bulky friend, standing with his hands on his hips. "Jimmy," he started. Robert didn't have to ask if it was running. He knew it was. But then he noticed there was no rebuilt muscle car in the space. He looked around him quickly, then back at Jimmy. "But where's the 'Bee?" He held his long hands upright at his waist, in a question.

"Ah, the 'Bee." Jimmy walked towards him now. "Sold it."

"Oh," Robert looked back at the truck.

"I was laid up a couple years ago. We needed some cash, so I took it to a show and sold it." Jimmy didn't sound upset but as if he had sold a load of hay. "Can't believe what I got for it."

"Well, it was beautiful." Robert pulled open the door of the cab and climbed in.

"It was, wasn't it?" Jimmy walked over and leaned against the open window of the truck. "And man, it could fly. But," he shrugged, "it was just a car." Jimmy pressed his lips together then. "I won't lie, it's been tough lately, Robert." Robert glanced up suddenly. Jimmy never complained about anything. "Been thinking about selling off that parcel over near the woods by the creek." Robert listened. He tried not to show how he felt because the truth was, he worried now about Jimmy and his farm. "It's not good for much, but someone might buy it, you know, just to have a hunting spot."

"You don't hunt?" Robert rested his arm on the window opening.

"It's only about ten or eleven acres. I'll still have plenty. And the cash would get me through the year. Be okay by then. Winter crops were good. Early planting went well. I think it's a good idea." That sounded like Jimmy was done talking about it, so Robert only nodded his head and looked around the cab of the truck.

Then Robert saw a key in the ignition. It didn't look familiar, and he realized, Jimmy had had to replace probably nearly everything on the truck. He looked at his old friend and shook his head. "I owe you."

"You always have," Jimmy smirked.

"No, really. I need to repay what you've put into this. I know parts aren't free."

"Depends where you get them." Jimmy patted the window opening. "Crank it up." He stood back. Robert pushed in the clutch and cranked the engine. It started immediately, of course. Robert would have bet money Jimmy had driven it today, just to be sure it was ready. Robert put the shifter in first and let out on the clutch and the truck jolted and stopped. He looked over at Jimmy, who started laughing hysterically. "Jeezus, Robert, you forgot how to drive?"

"Uh, new clutch, Jimmy." He wagged his hand in the direction of the pedal. There was more pressure when he pushed in the pedal, but in truth, it did feel a bit new to him, as if he were learning again how to drive. He started the truck again and let the clutch out more slowly.

"Don't burn it, Robert." Jimmy scolded in a yell, but there was a laugh in the statement too.

"Shut up, Jimmy," Robert teased back, and he pulled through the barn door into the light. The truck drove perfectly, and he quickly reminded himself of the driving. It seemed odd to have the recollection return so readily, the shifting, the gas, the braking. It was, he supposed, just another way he was back home again.

Out in the light, the truck looked even better. Jimmy had detailed the inside as well as the outside. Carla and Diana were putting the finishing touches on the food on the table, so Robert decided raising a cloud of dust by hot-rodding his old truck around the yard was not the best idea. But it sure ran great.

He parked near the FarmAll and walked over to the little table that was obviously intended as a serving spot rather than a dining table. There were paper plates in bamboo holders and plastic cups of ice. An opaque white plastic pitcher held lemonade with rounds of fresh lemon floating in it. A large Tupperware bowl beside the clear bowl of pasta salad held an array of sandwiches: cold cuts and lettuce on white bread. Another plastic bowl held what looked like vinegar slaw.

It was exactly the meal Robert would have expected. He decided this kind of filling, simple fare was much better than eating dandelions. His mouth watered. Jimmy came trotting up, rubbing his hands together and grinning at the array of food. "Let's eat," he said, but he did not take his eyes off the food. Diana shot a smile his way. "I'm starved." Then Jimmy looked over at her appreciatively.

Another day, Robert might have teased Jimmy that he certainly did not look starved, but he decided things were maybe not quite yet that casual again. Instead, he put his hand on Jimmy's broad shoulder.

"Here," Diana said, handing Robert a plate and a metal fork and a napkin. "You first, Robert." It was, in Robert's view, a way of saying, "We're going to get there. We will be just like old times again, and probably sooner rather than later."

But it was Carla who finally broke the ice as they ate, when she asked the question that probably was on the minds of everyone in Wyler's Ford. "Uncle Robert?" She looked up at him, her plate balanced on her lap as she sat tenuously on a bright blue chair. She held half a turkey sandwich, cut diagonally, in her hand. "Where'd you go?" Diana started a tiny bit, but Jimmy took another bite of pasta and looked at Robert, patiently waiting for his answer.

It was a fair question, Robert knew. He finished chewing his mouthful of salty ham, pickle, and mustard mushed between the fluffy bread. He wondered absently if he might forever be amazed at the things he took for granted before. He marveled how a simple sandwich could taste so delicious. As he swallowed, he thought how to best answer her. He looked at her, smiled, and shrugged slightly. "I went to heal." Carla just looked back, still holding her half-sandwich poised above her plate. She clearly was waiting for more than that. Robert looked at the ground, at nothing, really. "I didn't know that's where I was heading when I left. I just had to get away." He worried slightly at the tone of that. He looked up at Jimmy, who had stopped eating and was looking intently at him. "I didn't want to get away from you all, or Susan or Papa, or any of that. I think maybe I needed to get away from me." He cocked his head to one side. "Turns out, I didn't like myself very much, or at least who I saw when I looked in the mirror." He put his sandwich back on the plate in his lap. "When I lost Bobby, I wanted to blame the government and the army and just about everyone else. But the truth was, I blamed myself." He looked at Diana now, who was staring at him. "I felt I had led him to his death, that all the things we did together had ended up causing him to join up and become a ranger and go off to try to save the … world." He shrugged. He had wanted to use an expletive but had caught himself. "Out in the woods, I felt like he was there with me. I did all the things we used to do together and learned a lot more as well." He looked over at Jimmy, whose eyes were wet.

Robert did not want to make his story morose. It had been very sad, especially at first, but right now was not the time to go back there. He took a breath and deliberately brightened his tone, trying to sound as if he were describing a vacation he had taken, rather than the circumstances of his disappearance for over six years. "So, I went up Sugartop Mountain first. It's where we used to go backcountry camping, remember?" He nodded towards Jimmy, who dipped his head back in assent. "I just went up there and set up a primitive little camp like we used to do. I fished. I trapped a little. Then people started coming out when it got warmer and I decided to head down Triplett Branch, and then, I don't know, I just kept going, Carla." He bowed his head slightly towards her, and she kept her gaze steady on him. "I went all the way out to California before it was all said and done. Turned around and came back again."

"You walked to California?" Carla's eyes widened.

"No, not exactly. I walked. I hitchhiked. I met people who gave me a lift. I just sort of kept moving." Robert wagged his head.

"You ever hop a freight, Robert?" Jimmy shot him a smile. "Like we were going to do when we got in trouble in middle school that time?"

"Well, yes, a few times," Robert looked at the space between Jimmy and Carla, at the memory, then back at Jimmy. "Truth is, I did a lot of things I never, ever dreamed I would do." He looked up at Diana now. He wasn't sure just how much to tell, at first. "But I didn't do anything that would have shamed the memory of my son. I promise you that." He paused to think where to go next with a story of his disappearance.

Diana looked back at him, her eyes softer now. "Eat your lunch, Robert." She nodded towards his plate. "Sounds like maybe some tales for around the campfire, Jimmy." She looked over at Jimmy and whatever message was sent, Jimmy quickly gave a short nod of acknowledgement. Diana stood and put her half-full plate on the little table. She picked up the pasta and brought it over to Robert. "Have some more salad, Robert." She scooped out a large spoonful and plopped it on his plate before he could respond.

He had not intended to eat so much, but he knew this was more about Diana keeping things even. There would be the right time, she was saying. Robert took another bite of salad. He wondered if everyone thought he looked too skinny. Even at The Flintrock Grille, where he and Susan had gone for lunch after visiting the bank, the servings on his plate were half-again the portions on Susan's plate.

Everyone in the place stopped talking when he and Susan had entered, which was the way everyone usually acted when strangers came in, which they only rarely did. But then the place had erupted with talk, people pointing at the two of them, or, more accurately, at Robert. A few of them had the courtesy to come over and slap his back and say, "Hello, Robert. Good to see you."

But Robert didn't really mind, not nearly so much as Susan, who looked miffed at first that folks were acting different, but he told her it was all right. It was, in fact, natural for them to be surprised and curious and everything. It was he who had vanished, after all. But when the plates of meat and three arrived, Robert's pile of mashed potatoes with brown gravy overflowed the plate onto the plastic table cover. After that, Susan had calmed down. Actually, she laughed at the huge mound of food on Robert's plate. It was, they both knew, how folks in their hometown said they cared: they fed you.

The conversation lagged, then Jimmy spoke. "You're going to need to register the truck, Robert. Title is still in your name I expect." He waved absently with his fork. "Susan paid the taxes I think." Robert felt a humbling again. There was so much his family and friends had done for him while he was gone that he was probably never going to be able to repay, that they perhaps expected no repayment for, but he would. He would figure it out. He was full, but he took another fork of slaw. He didn't want to be rude. Carla watched him eating for several minutes, then she took another bite of her sandwich she been holding.

"You ought to write a book, Uncle Robert," she said after swallowing the bite.

Robert smiled. "I don't know. Maybe one day. I'm not sure I need to go back just yet, you know?"

Carla paused. "Yeah," she nodded. "Yeah, I get that."

"You're going to have to get insurance and so forth too," Jimmy continued on his train of thought.

"Yeah, that's right," Robert said. "I didn't think about that. You still use Jerry?"

Jimmy glanced quickly at Diana, who shot him a look at the same time. "No, we don't," he said tersely. He looked up at

Robert. "You don't need to go to him, Robert. I got a guy. I'll give you his name." Jimmy looked back at his plate to keep from looking at him. Robert puzzled over that exchange. They had been classmates with Jerry back in high school. He wondered just what might have happened. Evidently, even in Wyler's Ford, some things change.

When they had eaten, Carla brought out a carrot cake and served up pieces. Robert felt engorged. Then Diana started cleaning up and told Carla to help her, but Robert stood and said, "Let me." Carla sat and Robert carried piles of soggy paper plates and the nearly empty pitcher into the kitchen. Diana turned around from the refrigerator where she had placed the almost empty bowl of sandwiches. She took the plates from the holders which she stored in the pantry.

"Diana?" Robert stood in the center of the room, towering over her. She turned, a question on her face.

"Oh, just put the pitcher on the counter. I'll get it." She turned back around and tossed the stained, sagging plates into the trash can.

Robert placed the pitcher on the counter. "Diana," he said again. She turned now and looked up at him. "I'm sorry." Diana raised her chin. "I'm sorry for what I must have put you all through."

Diana turned and picked up the pitcher and started emptying it into the sink. "It was Jimmy, really, more than me." She was covering, and it showed in her tone. But Robert did not want to challenge her.

"Okay, but I'm sorry for what I put him through and, as a result, what I put you through. And Carla." Now Diana turned again and faced him.

"Okay, Robert. Okay." She walked over and hugged him around his middle. Then she backed up and looked at him again. "But don't you dare do that again, you hear me?" She shook her finger at him.

Robert couldn't suppress a grin. "Yes, ma'am." Then Diana grinned too, realizing how she must look.

"Go get the other bowls," she commanded, waving her hand towards the door. Robert left as ordered and retrieved the other items. That felt more like normal to him. It wasn't complete yet. It would take time. But it was definitely a start.

Carla left the two old friends to talk. Robert told Jimmy about seeing the attorney, about how it angered him for someone to take his property. They talked into the afternoon. Jimmy brought Robert up to speed on many of their old pals, although Jerry never came up. He decided he might ask his sister. Maybe she knew. He thought about mentioning the insurance money and how he was more than ready to reimburse Jimmy for all the money he must have spent on the truck, but remembered how his father had taught him a gentleman never discusses money, although the truth was, he and Jimmy usually talked about everything. Still, that could wait. And Robert would repay Jimmy.

Jimmy offered Robert a ride back to Susan's, but he needed to walk off the big lunch, so they put the truck and the old tractor back in the barn. Robert walked up the drive, his shadow growing longer in front of him, and wended his way back through the woods. He found himself behind his old house, where a light burned in the living room window. The place looked cozy.

He stopped for only a second, felt his stomach tighten in frustration, then pulled out his bamboo recorder from his pocket and played "We Three Kings" all the way to Susan's house. The sun was getting low in the sky when he arrived. He looked over the tall fence into her backyard. Susan was on her hands and knees, weeding the garden. He was struck by how much everything remained the same, yet everything was different. He went in to help with the weeding.

Chapter 11

Charlene pulled the car over in the dry dirt next to the road. A small cloud of dust rose as she pulled off the edge. Her little tan sedan didn't sound right all the way from the hairdressers. She hoped Terry might know what the problem was, but her faith in his automotive skills was not great. He was a good one for raising the hood on the car when she told him it was not running right, peering in as if he actually could tell anything from how the top of the engine looked, then throwing up his hands and saying, "You got me. Take it to the garage."

When she got out of the car, she could hear the engine ticking, like it was hot, maybe. It wasn't a sound it usually made. She wished they could get a new one, or at least a newer one. They had a little bit of money saved up. True, it wasn't a lot, but they had to get to work. They needed a reliable car. As far as that went, they really needed a second car so she wouldn't have to drop Terry off at the prison and pick him up at strange hours, since his shift often changed with the weekend coverage. If they got maybe a mini-van, Charlene could use it to go to the store and haul the kids around, Terry could drive the little two-door. Then he could come and go, and Charlene wouldn't have to pick him up at six in the morning, leaving the kids watching television for the thirty minutes or so it took to drive there and back. It was true, Luke was mature for his age, and he watched out for Rosie, but she still didn't love it.

Charlene bent over and looked under the car. Sure enough, something was dripping from beneath the car onto the dirt below. She straightened and gave out a sigh. It was a cool afternoon. Ditch lilies were almost ready to bloom on the other side of the road. Two crows called to each other from somewhere in the woods behind the house.

"Great," she said aloud. But Terry was inside, so maybe he could do his glance-at-it-and-declare-it-broken routine and then he could take it to the shop instead of her. It was the least he could do. Well, no, the least he could do would be nothing, but he would help.

She stopped at the mailbox beside the road before going in. The mailbox looked bedraggled. The red flag no longer went all the way flat anymore, and the front had some rust showing along the hinged corners. It had the number of their address on the post, but their name was not on the box. She opened the little door and pulled out the small pile of assorted flyers and junk and bills. She stood by the road, rifling through the mail.

The Piggly Wiggly weekly mailer was in there. She liked to look through that. It gave her ideas for suppers and, truth be told, she rather enjoyed going to the grocery. She would save that for later. There was a glossy advertisement for a home security system and what looked to be a notice about their health insurance. That was the best thing about Terry's job: they had coverage because of that. Being a guard at the privately run prison really didn't pay all that well, but the benefits were solid. Then she saw a letter from Martin Douglas, Attorney at Law. Terrence and Charlene Jeter and their address were neatly typed on the front, and the return address was printed in a fancy scroll on the back flap of the envelope. Charlene felt her stomach flip, then her whole body felt suddenly tired. She knew what it likely was. "Oh no," she sighed. She looked over at her sick little car as if its maladies were somehow to blame.

Charlene dragged herself into the house. Their house. It felt so familiar, so much like home. Terry was in the kitchen, his head and half his body scrunched up under the cabinet where the sink was. Charlene looked through the double-hung window in the dining area towards the back porch.

Rosie was scribbling carefully in a yellowed coloring book. Charlene had no idea where Rose had gotten it. Probably Terry had found it in one of the boxes of assorted junk they had put up in the attic crawl space. The crayons she knew: she had brought them home from Happy B's after the children there broke them or used them down to half their size. But there wasn't anything wrong with them: they still would color on a piece of paper. So rather than toss them out, Charlene had put them in an old coffee can and brought them home for the kids. They certainly never complained.

Farther out in the yard, Luke made a motion like he was firing an invisible gun from his hip. She couldn't hear him but could see his lips in the "skew" sound he made when he played army. He leaned back, as if absorbing the recoil of the rifle. Her stomach twisted again.

This had become their home. This had become their community. Only next week, the kids would be going to vacation Bible school over at Riverside Baptist, although neither she nor Terry went in for religion all too much. Still, it was free childcare for several weeks, even though Luke was probably not going to go in for gluing macaroni to a paper plate or making beaded necklaces. But he would be okay. He liked other kids to play with, so if the projects didn't interest him, the playmates would.

Now Rosie, she loved any kind of project. Charlene and Terry had a cardboard box full of assorted pieces of paper and notecards and who knew what all. True, most of them they could not discern now just what they were supposed to be, but nonetheless, they were projects Rosie had done. Luke usually tossed his after a few days. He never had had all that much interest in them. But wasn't the fact they were going to church a clear sign they belonged? she thought. She wondered if this Robert Younger guy even had a church. Maybe that was something she and Terry could use in their favor. She looked back at where Terry was struggling to tighten or loosen something under the sink. He grunted in effort. See, she thought, we're the ones fixing things here, not Younger. She might as well tell him the news, whatever it might be. Just getting the letter was bad news enough.

"Terry," she started.

Terry jumped and Charlene heard a deep "bong" from his head hitting on the bottom of the cast iron sink. She grimaced in sympathy. "Jeezus," he yelled. "Think you might give someone a little notice?" He crab-crawled out from under the sink. His tee shirt was sweaty and had a black streak across it. He held a crescent wrench in his right hand and rubbed his forehead with his left. "Dang, girl." He leaned forward into a sitting position. "You sure came in quiet-like." He was not all that angry. Charlene heard it in his voice.

"Sorry, babe." Charlene went over to the fridge and pulled open the handle that latched it shut. In the small freezer compartment, she reached for a bag of peas she knew was there. She felt it as much as saw it and pulled it out, squeezing the frozen pellets apart. She turned and handed it to Terry. "Here, Terry. Put this on it. It'll keep the swelling down."

"Okay," he put down the wrench, reached up, and took the bag. He sat on the floor, holding the bag of peas to his forehead. He stayed there a moment, letting the iciness work. "Yeah, I'd rather not go into the cell block with a big knot on my head. I don't want to give those guys any ideas." He reached up with his left hand and grabbed the sink, pulling himself to his feet. "Ouch." He blinked hard, the standing causing his dinged-up head to hurt more, perhaps.

"I'm sorry, Terry. I didn't mean to sneak up on you like that." Charlene went to him and although he was pretty sweaty, she put her arms around him and hugged him.

Terry hugged her back with just his left arm, then he leaned backwards and looked down at her. "What's the matter?"

Charlene didn't want to rush into the news about a letter from an attorney. Letters from lawyers had never been a good thing, at least in the Jeter world. "What do you mean? Why, is something the matter?"

"'Cause you never hug me when I'm all grimy like this. What is it, Charlene?" Terry took a step back and looked at her. She didn't want to let go of the hug because it meant telling him. She worried he might go off half-cocked or something, but he had pulled away, and she would have had to chase him across the room to keep up the hug, and there was no way that would be normal.

Then she remembered the car malfunctioning. That was bad enough news, but not as bad as getting the letter. "Car's acting up, Terry," she said as if, "yeah, you wheedled it out of me," but she knew she hadn't really sold it. "Something's leaking from underneath." She threw up her hands in defeat, her right hand still gripping the assorted mail.

"Oh," Terry bought it. "It's probably just condensation from the AC, hon." He leaned towards her with his arms outspread as if he was going to give her a big bear hug with his filthy clothes on. Charlene backed away this time. Terry really was very dirty. The bag of frozen peas looked ridiculous in his hand, as if he were going to give them to her as a present.

"Terry, it's a beautiful day. I didn't have the air on." She said it as if she were winning a debate. He grimaced.

"Well, hell. Let me take a look." He put the icy bag back on his forehead. She knew he had no idea what to look for. It was his usual man-thing to do; pretend he could gaze at a car engine and it would somehow heal itself. He started for the door and Charlene fell in behind him. She tossed the mail on the dining table and Terry glanced over at it reflexively, seeing the motion from the corner of his eye. But then he froze in his steps. Charlene looked over and saw the letter from the lawyer atop the pile. "What's that?" He waved his free hand at the stack.

"Mail?" Charlene tried to make it sound as if it was a silly question, but he was already turning to look at it. She just knew he was going to strip out a gear when he saw it, although the truth was, she had no idea what it said.

"No, this one." He picked up the official-looking envelope

from the table and looked at the front, flipped it over, and read the return address on the back. He tossed the bag of rapidly thawing peas onto the table, dropped the hand with the letter to his side, and let both shoulders droop. He looked up at the ceiling and breathed a deep breath. Then he looked over at Charlene. She read on his face that he knew what she had been doing, keeping the bad news from him. "Jeezus, Charlene." He looked back at the envelope and saw it wasn't open yet. "Think maybe this could be important, hon?"

Charlene hated sarcasm, but she could think of nothing to say. She just set her mouth in a straight line and hung her head. Terry took another breath and tore open the envelope along the top, using his finger as a letter opener, which made for a rough tear. He unfolded the letter and started reading. From where Charlene was standing, it didn't really look like a long letter, but Terry stared at it for what seemed like forever, perhaps rereading it a few times to get the full meaning.

"What is it?" Charlene went over towards him. He had a large bump rising on his forehead from banging it on the sink. She tried to act innocent, but figured she knew what the letter was.

"Goddammit," Terry dropped his hand to his side, still holding the letter. Charlene had to reach down to take it from him. She held it in both hands and read:

Dear Mr. and Mrs. Jeter:

Please be advised that you are trespassing on private property. Mr. Robert Younger, owner of the property at 1309 Willow Road, requests that you vacate said property within 30 (thirty) days of receipt of this letter to avoid further legal action, including but not limited to civil liability suits and prosecution of criminal actions. Mr. Younger is willing to drop all actions against you provided you vacate the property immediately. Please do not hesitate to have your attorney contact me if you have any questions.

Sincerely,
Martin Douglas, Attorney-at-Law

Charlene also read it twice, as if it might say something different the second reading. Then she looked up at Terry who was watching for her reaction, and she knew she had to try to be calm or he might go spewing off like a stepped-on cat. But this was not exactly what she had expected. She expected they would have to pay something.

"I thought we were going to get to stay here, Terry. You said the house was abandoned and if we just took care of it, it would become ours."

"Yeah, well, the son-of-a-bitch came back, didn't he?" Terry shook his head.

"Well, then, I guess we kind of thought this was coming, Terry." She tried to take an expression of calm. "We knew he was back. Where we going to go?" She couldn't help the sad look in her eyes she knew was there.

Terry looked at her incredulously. "Are you serious?" She looked back, trying to think of what to say. But it was too late. "No. If that goddamned lunatic thinks he can come in here and take our home from us, he's fucking crazy!" Terry yelled, turning away from her. Charlene glanced through the window and saw Rosie lift her head at the voice.

"Terry, please, the kids."

Terry spun around. "Yes, the kids. The kids, Charlene." He was full-throated now, his arms waving around. "What about our kids? What about our home?" He looked at her with his eyes bugging out.

"Well, dammit, Terry, I didn't do it." She wasn't really accustomed to cursing, so she kept her voice down. Terry stopped and looked at her.

"No," he said more quietly, looking at the floor. "No, of course not." Then he looked back at her. "But how can you not be pissed off at this?" He reached over, snatched the letter from her hand at her side, and shook it next to his face, crumpling the paper some. He was yelling again. His cheeks flushed, which matched the lump on his forehead. "This is our home, Charlene." He looked at her with his eyes filled with a confusion and fear she was unaccustomed to seeing in him. Terry was afraid and that was something he rarely was, even working at a prison. She studied him, and he went on, turning now to pace the small kitchen. "That crazy son of a bitch takes off. No one sees him in ages. And now he comes back, and everyone is supposed to bow down to him?" Charlene let him vent. What else could she do, she thought. "Goddammit." That sounded like desperation. "I ought to take a baseball bat to that crazy bastard and bash his skull in. Do the world a favor!" he bellowed.

Charlene looked through the window. Rosie was still leaning over the coloring book, but she was no longer scratching the crayon to paper. She was listening, pretending to be occupied with the drawing. Luke was sitting near her now, also pretending to be looking at the faded book, which he would have never been interested in. They knew something was up. They heard the yelling and, perhaps worse, the anxiousness.

Charlene looked back at Terry. She didn't like it when he lost his calm. "Well, that would be a good solution, Terry. You go ahead and attack that man and kill him and then they send you to the very prison you're working at. That should be fun. I mean, you would already have playmates, wouldn't you? And then where would the kids and I be?" She placed her hands on her hips.

Terry turned and looked at her. He lowered his voice now. "No, they'd send me to Eddyville for that." He gave a sad half-smile. "Even better playmates." He stood there quiet for a moment. She had managed to get him to quiet down, at least. The door opened and the kids came in, looking curious and a bit scared. Terry almost never lost his temper. They were unsure what it meant. They looked at Terry, then at Charlene, and although neither spoke, the question was clear: what's wrong? Terry glanced at them and blinked deliberately. He spoke to Charlene more quietly. "I've seen him around, you know."

"Who, Daddy?" Rose's eyes were wide.

Terry stooped down to make himself eye-to-eye with her. "That tall man you saw. Remember?" Rosie nodded. Terry stayed crouched down but looked up at Charlene. "I've heard him too, walking around in the woods playing Christmas songs in May on some daggum flute thing, which, I'd like to add, is not in tune." He stood now. "I'll bet he carved it out of some dead animal or something."

Charlene saw Rosie make a sour face imagining what that might mean. But Charlene had heard the flute too. She had not considered he might have made it himself. What an interesting thing to know how to do, she thought. But she doubted the dead animal part. That was just disgusting.

"I've seen him too, Daddy," Rose offered. "He hides in the trees sometimes."

Terry turned and looked at her. "Up in the trees?"

"No, he just stands there. He sort of looks like a tree, except he has pants on." Then she put her hand to her mouth and giggled as if she had said something naughty.

Terry looked at Charlene, then back a Rose. "Well, glad to know he has pants on." He opened his eyes wide in mock relief. This was more like the Terry Charlene had fallen for: level-headed, calm.

"I've seen him too," Luke said, not to be outdone.

Terry looked over at him curiously. "Yeah? Where?"

Luke shrugged. "Up in the woods?"

"Yeah? What was he doing?" Terry cocked his head to one side.

"He was just there, sort of." Luke shrugged again. He did a lot of that these days.

"Just there? What do you mean?"

"He was just there, and he helped me."

Terry shot a glance at Charlene but stayed calm. He stooped again to talk with Luke. "What do you mean he helped you?" Terry caressed Luke's arm.

"Um, well," Luke looked off to his right, towards the

ceiling, then back at his father. "I was lost, and he told me how to get home."

"Huh." Terry stood.

"Did he hurt you?" Charlene asked.

"No, Momma. He just told me which way to get home."

"He gave me some little strawberries to eat one time," Rose chimed in. "He said they are all over the place." She gave her mother an innocent smile.

Terry stood, turned, and looked at Rosie, then at Charlene. He blinked as if trying to make sense of the things he had just heard. Charlene wasn't sure what it meant either. Was this Younger guy mean or was he nice? She wasn't sure about her kids taking food from him, but Rosie had not gotten sick, so she guessed he must have given her something that at least wasn't poison. The room grew quiet.

"Bonnie's brother is a lawyer, Terry. Maybe we could ask him?"

"There's money we don't have to spend." Terry shook his head. "Besides, he does real estate things, doesn't he?"

"Yeah, but he's still a lawyer. And this is about real estate. Maybe we could just ask him, you know, like a consultation. I'll bet he wouldn't charge us anything for that."

Terry looked suddenly very tired. His arms hung limp at his sides and his face was drawn. "Yeah, I guess." There was defeat in his tone that Charlene didn't usually hear.

"It'll be okay, Terry." Charlene wanted to go to him and comfort him, like she would Rosie or Luke if they were sad, but she didn't want the kids to see him break down, and she had a feeling he wasn't too far from it.

"Yeah, I guess," he said, looking forlorn. Then he saw the children watching him closely and he made an almost physical effort to take on a more upbeat attitude. "Say," he said, walking over to the little table. "Who wants peas for lunch?" He picked up the bag and held it up as if he were a spokesperson on a television advertisement.

His ruse worked. "Ew, I don't like peas," Rosie whined

playfully.

"No, thanks," said Luke, shaking his head.

"You kids go play," Charlene shooed them out the door, her hands like a hen's wings, marshalling her chicks out of the way. They went out and Charlene turned to face Terry.

He was clearly trying very hard not to get down, but she knew. She knew he felt like a bad husband and a bad father because they might get evicted. He stood there, watching her, his face frozen in a blank expression that said he had no idea where to turn. The lump on his forehead was already getting bright red. He would have a mean bruise there in a day or two. Charlene wanted to change the subject, but she didn't know what new subject there might be. Then she said, "Want to come check on the car?"

"No, hon. Just take it to the shop." His face was almost devoid of any expression. "I can't fix anything." He sounded defeated already.

"You fixed the sink."

She saw the corners of his mouth turn up ever so slightly. "I did, didn't I?"

"Yes, you did." Charlene went to him now and wrapped her arms around him. He hugged her too, and they stood like that for what seemed like a long time.

Chapter 12

Susan read in the book she had picked out of the free library box beside city hall. It was a coming-of-age book that took place in the south. Susan was enjoying the read. Her attention was pulled through the window by Robert driving up in his truck in front of her house. The vehicle was fully legal now, insured and registered, and Susan was excited to see it again. Robert acted like an eighteen-year-old with his first car. He parked it on the street.

Susan put her book down to watch him get out of the cab and walk around the truck, admiring it. She had to chuckle. With his still too-blue jeans and his white tee shirt, he even looked like he did as a teenager. Then he turned and took the few steps with his long gait up to her front door and came in. She liked that he felt at home, but it was maybe just a little bit disconcerting he didn't knock. Or maybe she didn't want him to knock, but still there was a small sense of lost privacy, a privacy she had gotten quite used to. Robert ducked into the living room, grinning. That was another thing: yes, he was tall, but her doors were not so short he needed to stoop to get into the house. It wasn't like she was living in some sort of hobbit house.

"Hey, Suzy. Want to go out to the Dream Whip for a burger and a shake?" No one had called her Suzy since she was in middle school. He was just yanking on her rope a bit, she knew.

"Dream Whip? Wow, haven't been there in a while." She

117

let her thoughts skirt across the image. The Dream Whip had been the town kids' hangout for years. She liked the memory. "I think that's a great idea." Susan began unfolding herself from the wingback she sat in by the window, her "reading chair," she called it. One of these days soon, she was going to recover it, but as it was, it was wonderfully comfortable.

"Hey, great." Robert rubbed his hands together in anticipation. "You know, I was going to swing by there on the way here, but then I thought to myself, take Susan. She'll enjoy that."

Susan paused, gave him a sidelong glance, then stood to face him. "You know, I've always felt 'I thought to myself' is an odd redundancy. Of course you thought it to yourself. We all think to ourselves. We always do. Who else can we think it to? Unless you have unnatural telepathic abilities, it's guaranteed you thought it to yourself." She paused, watching the bemused expression cross his face. She went on regardless of his smirk while she slipped on her once-white tennis shoes. "I suppose it's a corruption of the similar, but yet different, expression, 'I told myself,' which makes ourselves both subject and object, so it has a strange perspective of its own. But 'I thought to myself' remains completely subjective, so it begs the question, if you thought it (clearly to yourself), why does that make it reportable?" She stood now and grabbed her small purse off the marble-top side table.

Robert was grinning at her now. "You know what? You need to get out more, Sis."

"I am out - all day." She headed towards the door, ignoring his insinuation. "I'm out in the garden, out in the garage, out on the porch . . ."

Robert fell in behind her, bending through the door. "No, you need to get out more around people."

Susan turned and looked at him with a smile. "Said the Goatman."

"Fair enough." He nodded.

Susan pressed her advantage. "So I should get out more

like going to the Dream Whip and sitting in my car?"

"Oh no, like going to the DW and sitting in my truck." He held up his keys and wagged them in the air.

Susan couldn't help but laugh. "Sure, why not?" They climbed in the truck and Susan was immediately aware of how clean and neat it looked. "Wow," she said, looking around her. "This sure looks good."

"Doesn't it? That Jimmy, I can't believe him." Robert cranked the starter and the truck hummed to life.

"Yeah." Susan put on the seatbelt. Even that looked cleaned. "Well, now you got it all spruced up, don't get it all muddy skinny dipping over in Jimmy's pond."

Robert gave out a guffaw. "What would you know about it?"

"You're funny, Robert. You think you're the only one who ever did that? Come on now." She waved her hand at Robert dismissively. Robert put the truck into first and drove down the lane.

He wore a smirk and shook his head slowly as if to say, "I should have guessed." After a couple of blocks, he twisted his head towards Susan and asked, "So, did something happen between Jimmy and Jerry?" He tried to keep the glance at her without taking his eyes off the road too much. "When I was out there, I said something about getting insurance for the truck from Jerry and Diana and Jimmy both acted strange, kept giving each other funny looks. They have a falling out or something?"

Susan was quiet for a moment, measuring her words. Then she said, "No, it's me. It's because of me they had a falling out."

"What?" Now he took his eyes off the road for a second and looked at her, his face concerned.

"Yeah, while you were gone, I worked for a while at Jerry's."

"Wait, did he try something? Did Jerry try something?" Robert's driving was suddenly a little erratic. "I'll take him apart starting with his ears and ending with his toes," Robert's voice rose.

Susan looked over at her brother, appreciative of his

protective attitude, but not really happy he grew so angry so quickly. "No, he didn't bother me, except, well, he did fire me."

"Fired you? What for?" Robert calmed himself.

"Uh, well, for cussing out one of our clients, or I guess, his clients." Susan gave a matter-of-fact lift of her shoulders, hoping that was the end of it.

Robert looked over at her, then back at the road. "Cussed out? That doesn't sound like you, Susan."

"Well," she shrugged.

"So why'd you do that? Who'd you cuss out? And why?"

"Okay, so it was Mrs. Chesterton. They own that big cattle farm across the river?"

"Yeah?" Robert urged her on.

"Well, she came in one day and said something I didn't care for, so I told her where to put it. End of story." Susan hoped her tone said, "That's all there is."

"I don't think so, Sis. What did she say?"

Susan waved him off. "Doesn't matter."

"I get the feeling it does." Robert just wouldn't let it go. It was always how he did things: pushing, pushing, pushing.

Susan was quiet for a moment. Then said with a sigh, "She said something cruel about you, okay? And I couldn't let it stand so I told her to shove it. Actually, I was very specific about where. Okay?"

Robert looked over at her as he drove up the main street. "That it?"

"Kind of. I couldn't understand why Jerry didn't say anything. He was supposed to be your friend, so I asked him right there, why he was such a cowardly dip-shit, or something to that effect."

At the one and only stoplight, Robert gave her a long sidelong look. "I'm guessing that was the straw that broke the back? That's pretty much when he fired you?"

"Yeah. I was so mad I could've bitten a cat. I decided to get something to plant. You know how digging in the dirt calms me down. So I went over to the hardware store and I saw Jimmy. We talked about it. He got nearly as angry as me." Susan looked at the floor mat of the truck, shiningly black.

Robert grew quiet, as if weighing what he had been told. "So Jerry just let the woman talk, huh?"

Susan blinked. "Yeah."

Robert read her tone. She sometimes hated how bad a liar she was. "Yeah, what?

"Well, he kind of made a joke about it, about what the woman said. I guess he thought it would put him in with the Chestertons or something. I don't know."

"What did she say?"

"It doesn't matter."

Robert thought about it for a moment, then said, "No, I guess not." He paused. "Wow. I guess some people can't wait to beat up on you when they can."

Susan looked over at her big brother, so strong yet so fragile. "Yeah, but at least now you know who your friends are."

He looked over at her and she raised an eyebrow. "My treat on the burger, Sis." He grinned.

"Okay, Daddy Warbucks." Susan gave him a warm smile. "But that'll cost you. I plan to get fries with that." He laughed.

They took their plain white bag of fast food and Robert drove off towards the outskirts of town.

"Where we going, Robert?" Susan stole a fry from the bag. They smelled delicious and she wanted to enjoy them still hot. If there was ever anything ruined by letting it cool down, it was a French fry..

"Oh, thought I'd enjoy my lunch at home," he said too nonchalantly.

"Ah, Robert. Really?" Susan folded up the top of the bag to hold the heat in. "Are you really going to go over and start something today?"

"No," Robert shook his head. "Just going to go park beside the road and have a picnic. Anything wrong with that?"

Susan could think of all manner of things wrong with it, including things escalating with Terry Jeter, who had been doing some talking at the prison about how he was going to fight leaving, how he was going to end up owning the place before it was over with. He had even dared to say he was not afraid of Youngers or anyone else, and if there was a veiled threat there, Susan didn't feel endangered. Sure, Jeter had some training to be working at the prison, although not much. Guards were notoriously undertrained and underpaid there. And Robert had always been handy with his hands, with his reach being his main advantage. But that didn't mean Susan wanted any of that to happen. In fact, she really couldn't see a positive outcome if the two men came to blows.

Robert parked the truck just up from his house. Susan figured he would have parked directly in front of the place, except the two children were playing in the yard and maybe Robert thought better of starting something. The Jeters' car wasn't there, but the little boy and girl were hopping around the yard, playing what looked to be a form of freeze tag.

Susan carried the bag of food back to the tailgate, which Robert lowered. Susan hopped up to sit on the gate. Robert simply sat down on it. Susan tried to enjoy her lunch, but the anxiousness she felt just being there plus the now-cooling fries made her stomach queasy. She couldn't help shaking her head. She had an overwhelming feeling something bad was about to happen.

Meanwhile, Robert sat munching away merrily, as if he truly were just on a picnic. He took a bite of the burger, then watched the kids playing. The two children had seen them, of course, pausing in their play long enough to gawk at them a moment, then went about their play as if two strange people weren't sitting down the road in the back of a pickup truck eating lunch. It was, she thought, as if they recognized her and her brother. Or at least her brother.

Robert reached into the sack and pulled out several greasy potato strips and ate them. Then he stopped chewing. He was staring at the kids, who were now much louder. Susan looked up and saw the little girl was in fact crying and screaming while the boy was thrashing at something at the edge of the woods, swinging his arm back and forth, darting forward, then back.

"Oh, shit." Robert put his burger on the truck bed, still half-wrapped in waxed paper. Susan looked back at the kids. The boy was stumbling backwards now, kicking. A ribbon looked to be tied to his lower leg, but then Susan saw what it was: a snake had struck at the boy's calf.

Robert took off at a sprint. The children's mother came out on the porch, poised behind the screen door as if she were going to simply check on the commotion then return to whatever chore she might have had interrupted by the noise. Susan dropped her burger onto the tailgate and raced after Robert, but he was there before she even made the road.

The boy was howling now, the little girl screeching a long, single high note only children can hit, her eyes wide with terror. Susan saw Robert step on the body of the snake on the ground as soon as he reached the boy.

He reached down with both hands and grabbed the head and the tail of the bright brown viper. By the time Susan arrived, Robert was turning like a discus thrower and heaving the snake across the road and into the trees, the beast spiraling and writhing as it flew through the air. It landed in the woods with a thumping crunch of leftover leaves from last fall.

Robert bent over the boy now. The mother had scurried out and run over to the boy, the back of one hand to her mouth that looked very much like it needed to scream but could find no voice. The little girl was still emitting the siren scream, her face turning red.

Robert was leaning over the boy, but he was looking towards the woods. Susan followed his eyes and saw the small knife lying at the edge of the yard. The mother came now to the boy's side.

"Oh my God, Luke," she panted. She reached for the boy, but Robert was already looking at the two neat holes in his calf.

"You trying to kill that snake, boy?" Robert's voice was low, surprisingly calm.

"Yes sir. It tried to get Rosie and she's afraid of snakes, so

I was going to kill it."

"Oh, Luke," Charlene fluttered her hands around the boy's face. She was bent over the child now and looked at Robert. "Tell me it wasn't poisonous," she gasped.

"Timber rattler, Ma'am."

"Oh my God!" the woman screamed.

Robert turned his head and looked at her in disbelief. "It'll be okay," he said calmly. Now the boy started squirming as his mother tried to wrap him in her arms. Robert blinked twice.

"Can you get the poison out, mister?" the boy yelled. "Please get it out." He thrashed his foot as if he could maybe kick the poison out of himself.

"Okay, now stop," Robert commanded, but his voice was still calm, even. The boy did stop and looked up at him. "You need to stop kicking. Calm down. Jumping around will only make things worse." He looked at the mother. "Go get your purse, insurance cards and such." He waved her towards the house. She looked blankly at Robert for just a second, then took off at a gallop that surprised Susan in its speed. Robert looked back down at the boy. "The best thing is for them to give you some medicine. They have something they can give you that keeps the poison from hurting you. It's called an anti-venom. That snake put venom in you; the doctors can make it so it doesn't hurt you. You understand?" The boy nodded. "If you move around too much, you just make the venom move around in you, and that's not helpful, so just lie still. Okay?"

"Yes sir." The boy was clearly terrified, but Robert's command of the circumstances quelled the thrashing. Susan looked over at Rosie, as her brother had called her. She had stopped the ear-splitting scream and now stood motionless, her face crimson, eyes opened very wide, tears streaming down her face.

"Did the snake bite you, honey?" Susan didn't think it had but wanted to be certain. She went over and stood by the girl to comfort her, and the girl wrapped herself around Susan's waist.

"No," the boy answered for his sister. "I heard and I seen

the snake and told Rosie to run away. He didn't get her." Susan could hear his pride in his voice. The mother came running from the house now, her too-large purse draped over her arm and banging against her side as she ran.

"Miz Jeter?" Robert glanced over at her when she stood panting from exertion and terror beside them. She acknowledged him by simply stopping and paying attention. "We need to get the boy to the hospital over in Morehead."

The mother reached into her purse and pulled out her cell phone. "I should call an ambulance." She fumbled with the phone, her hands shaking. She could barely hold the phone, much less push any button.

"No," Robert said, clearly trying to mete out his message calmly. "No time to wait for them. We need to get him there right away." He looked back at the boy's leg that was already beginning to get red. He looked back at the woman. "You okay with my sister here staying with your girl? You and I can take him in my truck." Robert looked over at Susan, who simply nodded her acceptance of the plan.

The woman looked at Rosie, then at Susan, then back at Robert. She was clearly torn.

"We'll be fine, Miz Jeter," Susan reassured her, and with the girl still tightly grasping her waist, they looked as natural as a vine growing around a tree.

"Okay," the mother gasped. "Okay," she said again. "Rosie, I am going to the hospital with Mr. Younger. You stay here with, um, . . ." She paused.

"Susan," Susan filled in the space.

"You stay with Susan and Mommy will be home soon, okay?"

The little girl looked at her mother now with wide, terrified eyes, but she nodded her head "Yes."

The mother stepped forward to get Luke, but Robert was already lifting him up as if picking up a rag doll.

"Let's go, boy. You'll be okay." Robert walked quickly but somehow unhurriedly to the truck and Mrs. Jeter had to run to catch up to them. "You get in first, Miz Jeter. I'll put him on your lap. Keep him calm. Keep his head raised." The mother managed to race ahead and climb into the truck ahead of them. Robert reached the boy across his mother's lap. "Call your husband on the way. Tell him it's alright, but to meet us at the hospital."

Susan watched Robert step around the back of the truck to climb in the driver's side, and she saw Mrs. Jeter twist in her seat to watch him make his way. Her expression seemed somewhere between gratitude and disbelief. Robert climbed in, started up the engine, then took off down the road, splashing through a wet spot that was a puddle even on the driest days. The white paper bag and their sandwiches slid off the open tailgate and tumbled into the road.

Chapter 13

Robert reached across Mrs. Jeter and took Luke from his mother's lap. The boy barely weighed anything. Robert carried him into the ER. He had had the mother, "Charlene" she told him to call her, phone ahead, and she was told a doctor would be waiting for them. All the way to the hospital, he had reminded Charlene to keep the boy's head elevated. She cooed at the boy and reassured him, but Robert wasn't sure whether the statements of "You'll be fine" and "It's okay" were meant for the boy or for Charlene herself.

She had also called her husband and had clearly tried to stay calm, but her voice quaked the entire conversation with him. "Terry? No, honey. Yeah, so listen. Lukie's been bit by a rattler." She had looked down at the boy, who already was showing signs of drowsiness, his eyes lolling back in his head. Robert made sure he showed calmness, but he was worried for the boy. He drove faster. He was a skinny kid, and it was a good-size snake. "No, I think he's going to be just fine." That was clearly meant for the boy. "Just meet us at the hospital in Morehead, okay? We're on our way there now." She paused, listening. "Um, no, Mr. Younger is taking us." She paused again. "Honey? Honey?" The second "honey" was louder. There was another pause. "Just get there, okay? Hurry," she said in a more exasperated tone. Then she pushed the disconnect button quickly, effectively hanging up on her husband, Robert thought.

"Put him over here." The doctor who met them at the door pointed at a gurney with a crisp white sheet on it. He looked far too young to actually have attended medical school, much less graduated, but then, Robert figured that probably had more to do with Robert's age than the doctor's, as well as the fact Robert hadn't actually seen a doctor in, well, at least six years. He had never been that big on going to a doctor. It was, perhaps, something he got from his own father. Perhaps it was time he got a checkup, but not right away, not just yet.

Robert carried the child over and put him down. There were two thin streams of drying blood across his calves. Two nurses, one a woman, the other a man, began loosening the boy's clothing and cleaning the spot where he had taken the bite.

Robert stood back to watch what they were doing to care for the kid, but another nurse came up to him and regarded him thoughtfully for just a second. "We'll take it from here, Papa," she said reassuringly and patted his chest with both hands. Robert looked down quickly. He considered correcting her but decided it just wasn't important in that moment.

The nurse led him backwards for a step by blocking his path, then abruptly yanked a white curtain before him, blocking his view. The metal rings on the curtain shrieked. The room smelled of disinfectant and something unidentifiable but definitely unpleasant. The fluorescent bulbs hummed and gave out a blinding blue-white light. Robert looked over at Charlene who stood staring at the curtain. Her mother's instinct told her it was bad, Robert figured. She was frozen in fear and indecision, except for a vague tremor through her entire body.

"Let's go sit in here," Robert said, pointing towards the small waiting room filled with molded plastic and chrome chairs and mismatched tables with haphazard stacks of ripped and battered magazines. An older man was sitting along the wall, covered with a ratty quilt, coughing. No one else was there. "They'll take care of him." A part of Robert felt relief to be handing off the boy to the doctors and he immediately felt a pang of guilt for that feeling. "Your husband should be here directly."

Charlene didn't move. She continued to stare at the white curtain. He put his hand on her shoulder to gain her attention and she let herself be led to the waiting room. Now, as she shuffled towards the seating area, her eyes seemed focused on something far removed. Robert had to lead her to a chair. She turned and sat, and, as if sitting brought her out of her stupor, she looked at Robert, her eyes wide and filling with tears.

"He's gonna die, ain't he?"

"No, he's not." Robert felt the shock of her question. He didn't know if the boy would die, but he could not bring himself to lay any doubt on her now. She was one piece of bad news from becoming a patient at the hospital herself, he figured. Robert had certainly seen grown men, bigger, stronger than this boy, succumb to snake bites. But he also knew children sometimes have a resiliency adults do not. And those men had not gone to hospitals. The boy was getting better care. The look in her eyes told him she was not sure she believed him. He reached around and put his hand on Charlene's shoulder and pulled her into a sideways rest against his side. She let herself be comforted. She leaned against Robert and sniffled quietly, staring at the floor.

The husband came in from the parking lot, letting his eyes scan the room until he saw Charlene resting against Robert. Robert saw him come in, his blue uniform shirt wet under the arms in big circles. When Jeter saw them, his face took on a look of anger and confusion. He marched towards them, his arms cocked and swinging back and forth as if he were a sweaty soldier in a parade in some tin-pot country.

Robert wondered just what the man might be considering. What he needed to be considering was the well-being of his son, but if he needed to be put in a gurney right next to the boy, this was certainly the logical place for that to happen. Robert stiffened his back and Charlene sat up straight.

"Terry," she jumped up and met her husband before he got to them, putting her hands on his chest. She saw her husband's aggressive posture too. Robert sat looking as calm as he could, but he was also keeping his eye on the man. Robert nonchalantly moved his feet below the chair in case he needed to stand quickly, but he also did not want to seem either intimidated or antagonistic. Charlene tried to lead her husband away. "Terry, thank God you're here. Lukie's in there now."

She took a hand off his chest and pointed towards the room next to them with several curtained areas within, where they had left the boy. But Jeter didn't move. He stood there glowering at Robert. Then he looked down at Charlene and back at Robert.

"Just what the hell is going on here, Charlene?" He slowly cocked his head in both a question and an accusation. Charlene's eyes widened and then her face scowled immediately. Evidently, she believed her husband was simply waiting for an opportunity to confront Younger, but this insinuation she had not expected. She paused for just a second, letting the sting of his suggestion sink in. She looked like she was ready to pop.

Now Charlene dropped her other hand from his chest, and she took a step back. "You stupid ass," she snarled. "Your son is in the next room dying from a goddamned snake bite and if he manages to live, it will only be because Robert here," she pointed at Robert, and Robert heard her very deliberate use of his first name, "got us here to the hospital in time to maybe save Luke's life." Now she was shouting. Jeter's face paled. The old man parked under the quilt at the edge of the room coughed, perhaps reminding them all he was still there. Charlene's sudden anger surprised Terry. "What the hell do you think is going on here, Terry?" She paused, as if waiting for an answer, but the question seemed unanswerable to Robert. Jeter had made it clear in his tone what he supposed, and Charlene had just as quickly dowsed that supposition.

Terry turned now, focusing on the room she had pointed to, and perhaps trying to change the subject to what he should have made the subject from the beginning. "Where's Luke?"

"Like I said, he's in there," Charlene put her hands on her hips. She was clearly not over his suggestion she had somehow been fooling around with Robert or anyone. Robert sat quietly, as if watching a scene from a soap opera unfold before him. He no longer felt Jeter was a threat to create an altercation there in the ER waiting room.

Terry glanced back at Charlene. "Well, what're they doing?" His tone was one of exasperation, but he was still uneasy in the aftermath of Charlene's anger.

"Well, I hope to God they are saving his life." Charlene was beginning to bring her fire under control as well. There was, obviously, a much more immediate concern.

"Where's Rose?" Terry's eyes darted back and forth from the ER to Charlene.

"She's at home," Charlene measured her words. Terry's eyebrow shot up, curious.

"My sister's with her," Robert said slowly, calmly.

Jeter's face screwed up again in confusion. He glanced at Robert, then back at Charlene. "His sister?" He shook his head.

"There wasn't room in the truck," Robert offered.

"Lukie's bit bad, Terry." Charlene brought the attention back to her son. Terry paused, then spun on his heels.

"I'll see what's going on. Let me handle this." He marched away towards the ER. Robert wondered if he always swung his arms that way or if it was intended to portray something to people, like Jeter was somehow the man in charge. The huge rings of sweat under his arms betrayed maybe less control than he wished for. It seemed ridiculous to Robert. What the man should have been in charge of is teaching his boy to leave a snake alone and it won't bother you. It seemed to Robert that maybe Jeter himself didn't know how to behave in the woods. But then, maybe that was not totally fair. Robert had, after all, pretty much made it his life's work to be that guy, especially over the last several years. In truth, even in the mountains out west where he had met a number of avid outdoorspeople, few were as at home in the wilderness as he was.

While Terry stomped off, Charlene turned and gave an apologetic look at Robert, but Robert just gave her a small smile and a nod to say, "It's okay. Don't worry about it." Soon, Terry came back with the baby-faced doctor walking beside him, his hands tucked into the pockets of his white jacket. Robert decided that it was at least something that Jeter had managed to bring back someone who might spread some light on the well-being of the boy. Perhaps he did have a little bit of effective assertiveness.

"Good afternoon," the doctor said, smiling. "We are preparing the antivenom vials in our pharmacy now." He was pleasant but matter-of-fact. Robert could not say he disapproved. Get to the heart of the matter. "And you're the one who brought him in?" He nodded towards Robert.

"Yes, his mother and I." Robert stood now, and the doctor watched him rise to tower over him a bit, but he was not particularly taken aback. Robert liked that as well. The doctor glanced back and forth between Robert and Terry, curious. "I'm a neighbor," Robert offered. Terry started visibly.

The doctor kept bobbing his head. "I see. And you saw the snake?"

"Yes."

"He took the snake and chucked him deep into the woods, is what he did," Charlene chimed in appreciatively. Terry took his eyes off the doctor to look at Robert, as if sizing him up.

"And you're certain it was a rattlesnake." If the doctor noticed any of these reactions, he ignored it.

"Oh yes. Timber rattler, about four feet long." Robert held out his arms to demonstrate, adjusting it as he measured with his eyes, so he looked a little bit as if he were playing an invisible accordion.

"I see. Good to know. We will give the boy . . ."

"Luke," Terry interjected.

"Right, we'll give Luke a dose of the antivenom. If he responds well to the initial dose and he has no allergic reaction, then we will give him two additional doses every six hours for three more doses. Ninety percent of patients start to improve after that regimen. Most of the remaining patients show improvement after maybe four to six more injections. The antivenom works well. We experience an almost one hundred percent recovery rate." Charlene let out a deep long breath that sounded as if she had been holding it for a very long time. She looked as if she might buckle at the knees, and Robert worried she might actually collapse, but then Terry turned and held her.

"Thank you, doctor," the husband managed, holding up his wife.

"Well, it's a good thing you got him here so quickly. The sooner we start the treatments, the better. Please let me know if you have questions." The doctor gave them a pleasant if perfunctory smile, then spun and walked back into the ER.

Terry looked up at Robert, an expression of gratitude and a small, thin smile on his face. Robert gave a nod back to say, "You're welcome." There was an awkward moment of silence. Then Robert stepped back. "I'll go check on Susan and the girl," Robert offered. He was glad the hospital was there, that they were taking care of the kid, but the less time he spent there, the better, as far as he was concerned.

"Rose," Terry corrected, as if a rote response, then he looked again at Robert. "Rosie, we call her." He helped his wife to a seat, and she plopped back into the chair, seemingly exhausted. Terry turned and faced Robert now, looking up at Robert's chin. The two men stood there for a moment, silent, then Terry said, "I don't know what to make of you, Younger." Charlene looked up at them, but she was clearly not worried about the two men now. "Beginning to think you ain't as broke as folks made you out to be." At that, Robert had to smile. Terry went on, "Still don't know what to think of you hanging around my family."

Robert let his smile weaken to a more wistful smirk. "Well, your family is in my house, Jeter. Bound to happen." Terry didn't respond and Robert walked away, out the door and over to his truck. He climbed in and saw a bloodstain in the cloth bench seat from where the boy had bled.

No, not "the boy." Luke.

Chapter 14

Rosie held on to the woman with all her might, but it also felt funny. She didn't know the woman, and it wasn't at all like holding on to Mommy. Mommy was softer than this lady, who was taller and thinner and even wore blue jeans like Daddy did when he was at home. But Mommy had said to stay with the woman.

Susan was her name. Rosie liked that name. If the woman wasn't as soft as Mommy, she thought her name was soft and that counted for something. And she liked her hair. It was long and yellow, and she had it pulled back in a ponytail. Rosie liked ponytails. She wished she had a ponytail.

She watched the truck growl down the road with Lukie, Mommy, and the giant all inside. Rosie was afraid for Lukie and a little bit for Mommy, but she wasn't really sure why she was afraid for Mommy. Maybe it had to do with her going off with the giant who scared Rosie some, if for no other reason he was so big. Rosie held on to Susan a few more minutes until she felt a little less afraid, and maybe not so sure the snake would come back and bite her.

Then the woman reached down and untied the knot Rosie had made of her hands around the woman's waist. She stooped down so that she was looking right into Rosie's eyes, which still felt wet from crying, but she wasn't crying now. That was something Daddy did too, bending over to talk with her. Rosie liked that too.

"Your brother's going to be okay," the woman said in a soft, scratchy voice, her hands on Rosie's shoulders. "And we're going to be okay." She nodded now to Rosie, and Rosie thought Susan must know if it would be okay because she said so, and she wouldn't say so if it weren't true. "Okay?" the woman asked, and Rosie nodded her head. She wanted it to be okay and maybe if she said it would be okay too, it would be true. "Maybe we can go sit on the porch and wait a bit, okay? I think it may be a while."

Susan stood and took Rosie's hand in hers. Susan's hands were long and thin and that too was different from Mommy, whose hands were rounder and kind of stubby. Rosie walked with Susan towards the porch, but she was looking at Susan's hand that was holding her own. She held the back of Rosie's hand with her thumb, just barely enough pressure to keep their hands together.

The two of them walked over to the porch and sat on the edge. Rosie often sat right there, coloring in one of the books with grey-brown paper that had come from the attic. The one she was coloring in these days had pictures of elves making shoes, while a shoemaker slept in a bed that was in the very same room as the bench where they were making shoes. Rosie always wondered why the hammering of the nails into the bottoms of the shoes, which is what one picture was, didn't wake up the shoemaker, but she had decided maybe it was because they were elves and they knew how to hammer without making any noise.

Susan sat next to her on the edge of the porch. Her knees were almost up to her chest, but she didn't seem to mind. In fact, she put her arms around her knees now and leaned forward and looked very much like she was okay sitting like that. Rosie looked at how Susan was sitting, then pulled her legs up on the porch where she sat, and she put her arms around them the way Susan did. Then she rested her chin on her knees. She liked the way it felt, to be sitting like Susan, who smiled down at her now.

"Is Lukie all better now?" Rosie asked, her chin bobbing

atop her knees.

"He will be," Susan said, and then she leaned over and rested her chin on her knees just like Rosie was doing. Rosie decided they looked just alike, sitting there on the porch, huddled like little toy monkey dolls. "My big brother? The one who threw the snake way, way out into the woods? He's really smart about the outdoors. He always knows just what to do."

"You mean the giant?" Rosie tried to look at Susan when she spoke, but it was hard to look up and keep her chin on her knees, so she sat up straighter. Now Susan laughed.

"Yes, the giant." She laughed again. "He's not really a giant, you know," she stopped laughing. "He's a man, just like your daddy. My brother's just really tall." Susan wasn't resting her chin on her knees anymore either, and when she talked, her ponytail swung back and forth.

"Okay." Rosie watched Susan's hair swishing back and forth as she spoke and nodded to Rosie. She just loved ponytails. "Susan?" Rosie asked. She hadn't said her name aloud and she liked the way it sounded. She liked saying her name. She thought about maybe just saying it over and over, maybe five or eight times, just because it was a pretty name, but she didn't.

"Yes, Rosie?" The woman turned her head to see Rosie's face and her hair flipped again, wonderfully.

"Can we put my hair in a ponytail like yours?" Rosie hoped the answer would be yes. That would make her so happy.

Susan smiled at her. "I don't see why not." Rosie let herself make a big wide grin. Susan stood now and reached into her pocket of her jeans. "In fact, I even have," she stopped talking while she fished in the pocket, "another hair band right here." She pulled out a small springy circle of blue lace. "I'm always losing these." Susan put the band around her four fingers of one hand. "Okay, turn around."

Rosie was so excited she could barely sit still. She forgot all about the snake. She spun around on the porch, so her back was to Susan. Susan pulled Rosie's curly clump of messy hair back gently over and over until it was a ponytail. Then Rosie felt the band go onto her hair. "There," Susan said. Rosie turned around to look at Susan. She could feel the ponytail flip behind her.

"Oh, thank you, Susan," Rosie swished her head back and forth to feel the sway of the hair.

"Careful, you'll make it come loose." Susan smiled at Rosie. Rosie thought maybe Susan was her new best friend. This is what best friends do, wasn't it? she thought. Make each other happy and do fun things together? Yes, this Susan was okay. Rosie stopped wagging her head and just sat there a moment, feeling a lot happier now that Lukie was going to okay, and now that she had a new friend.

As she sat there being very glad, a crow landed in the yard not far from them. "Look," said Rosie. "That's a crow, Daddy says."

"That's right." Susan looked at the bird too, and the bird started strutting around the yard in his funny walk, his head and body going this way and that way. Rosie thought he looked very funny, and she started laughing.

"Look at him." Rosie pointed at the bird who didn't seem to care at all that she and her new friend were sitting there. "He walks funny."

"He does, doesn't he?" Susan looked over at the bird and smiled, but she didn't laugh. Then she stood up and the crow flew off. Susan put her arms down straight at her sides and started walking around in a circle like the crow had. She leaned her body back and forth just like the bird. "Look at me," she said. "I'm a crow." Rosie giggled at Susan being a crow. She thought that was a wonderful game.

Rosie stood now and put her hands in her armpits. She bent her knees and flapped her arms like wings and said, "Guess what kind of bird I am, Susan." She walked forward and stopped and used one foot to act like she was scratching the dirt. Then she said, "Buck, buck, buck."

"You're a chicken," yelled Susan, pointing at Rosie. Rosie clapped her hands. "Now me," Susan said. "Guess what kind of bird I am." She put her arms down against her sides but bent her hands so they were sticking out. Then she barely moved her legs and waddled around in a little circle.

"You're a penguin!" shouted Rosie, pointing at her friend. She decided this, in fact, might be the best game ever.

"That's right," Susan stopped and clapped her hands together. She seemed to like the game too. It was true Susan wasn't a little girl like Rosie, but she was fun. If there had been any girls around this area Rosie's age, they wouldn't be any more fun than Susan, Rosie thought. "Now it's your turn, Rose." Rosie thought about what bird to be.

Then she remembered the ones she had seen out by the tool shed. There were two of them, and they liked to fly into the big pine tree. Rose leaned forward, her arms in her pits to be wings. She looked at Susan from the side of one eye, then turned her head to look at her using the other eye. Then Rosie moved her head back and forth and she said, "Ooooo, oo, oo."

Susan clapped her hands together again and laughed out loud. "Oh, my goodness, Rose. That's the best mourning dove I've ever seen." Rosie stopped being a bird and stood still, looking at Susan. She wondered when she ever had so much fun with a grown-up.

"Hey, Susan, you want to see my room?" Rosie opened her eyes wide. She really hoped the answer was yes. Maybe they could play dress-up, except there weren't any clothes for Susan to dress up in. Maybe make-up. Rosie would bet anything Susan would be great at a make-up party.

But Susan turned her head slightly and looked like she was thinking about something, then said, "I don't know, Rose. I'm not sure that's a good idea. Your mother didn't say anything about going inside."

"Mommy," Rosie corrected.

"I'm sorry?" Susan raised an eyebrow.

"Her name is 'Mommy,'" Rosie explained.

"Ah, I see." Susan nodded. Rosie was disappointed Susan wasn't coming inside, but it was true Mommy hadn't said she could. "You know what, Rose? I would love a glass of water.

Could you go get us both a glass of water?"

"Sure." Rosie liked that she could get some water for her friend, and now that she thought about it, she was thirsty too. She turned and jumped onto the porch and went through the screen door which banged shut behind her as she darted in. This was fun too, getting water for herself and her friend. It was maybe not as fun as a make-up party, but it was still fun.

She used a chair to get two metal glasses from the cabinet. One was green, the other purple. Purple was Rosie's favorite color, but she decided Susan could have it just this once, since she was a new friend. The cups curled outwards at the top and the green one had a small dent where it had fallen from the dishrack once, but she didn't care. She climbed down and scooted the chair over to the sink and stood on it to fill the glasses as full as she could. Then she pushed the chair back and picked up the cups and headed for the front door where Susan was.

The glasses were very full, and Rosie's hands weren't very big, so the water sloshed out some as she walked, but she kept going, focusing on the tops of the cups as she walked. When she reached the screen door, she turned and pushed it open with her back. Susan was sitting on the edge of the porch again, where they had sat before, except she wasn't holding her knees. She reached over for a cup and Rosie handed her the purple one. She hoped Susan would like it.

"Thank you, Rose." Susan took a drink of water and Rosie did too. She didn't realize just how thirsty she was. She took a long drink. When she lowered the cup, she could feel the water moustache on her upper lip, so she wiped it off with the sleeve of her shirt. Susan was just sitting there, looking around the yard, first at this, then at that. Then she turned to face Rosie. "Rose?"

"You can call me 'Rosie,' if you want. It's what all my friends call me." Rose took another drink, but not as much this time.

Susan kept looking at Rosie. Her mouth smiled a little bit, but her eyes smiled a lot. "Okay, Rosie it is," she said. "So, tell me, Rosie. How do you like living here?" Susan raised her chin.

Rosie put her cup down on the porch next to her, just like

Susan had. "It's okay, I guess. There's not as many fun stores to go to here as there are at Grandma's house, but kindergarten was fun. My best friend is named Tiara. She lives in town."

"Tiara," Susan opened her eyes wider. "Now that's a pretty name too, almost as pretty a name as Rosie." Rosie felt a little embarrassed.

"And Susan," she suggested. Now Susan laughed.

"I never really thought about it. Know what my big brother used to call me?"

"What?"

"Suzy. You can call me Suzy, too, if you want."

"Suzy Two?" Rosie cocked her head to one side. "Who is Suzy One then?" Now Susan opened her eyes even wider, then she laughed loudly and even slapped her pants leg once.

"Oh my," Susan gasped. "You are a riot, Rosie."

Rosie grinned. She realized she had misunderstood, but she was glad it was just a really funny joke. Suzy had a nice laugh. Rosie sat there a moment, just enjoying the fun she was having with her new friend.

Then Suzy caught her breath and said, "How do you like living here, in this house, Rosie?"

Rosie looked around her, sizing up the place. It had always been where she lived, as far as she knew. Daddy and Mommy said she was born in West Virginia, but she had no memory of ever being there. "It's okay," she allowed. "I wish I had my own room, like Tiara has. I like Lukie, but I wish I had my own room." Then she remembered about what happened earlier. "I don't like snakes. This house has snakes."

"Well, the snake wasn't in the house, was he?"

"No," Rosie allowed. "But Daddy says we need to be careful because of them."

"That's true," Suzy nodded. She picked up her cup and took another drink. Rosie picked hers up as well.

"I like being outside though. Being outside is more fun than being inside." Rosie took a sip of water. She felt a little sloshy from her big drink before.

"You know, my brother would absolutely agree with you," Suzy said. Rosie thought about that. It made her wonder about Suzy's tall brother, who it turned out was not an actual giant, but just really tall. Then she remembered the coloring book she had been coloring in earlier.

"Hey, Susan? I mean, Suzy?"

"Yes, Rosie?" Suzy answered, but she was looking around the yard, still sitting on the porch, but looking all around.

"You want to color in my coloring book?" Rosie felt excitement at having someone to color with. Lukie used to color with her, but anymore, he didn't want to color in the book but used the crayons to draw pictures of cowboys and Indians on the back of papers Mommy brought home that had stuff printed on the other side.

Susan looked at her now. "You know what? I think that is a great idea." She nodded her head once as if to say she really meant it.

"Great!" Rosie yelled as she stood and ran into the house. She brought out the one she had been coloring in before and the round cardboard box oatmeal had come in that was now full of all sorts of crayons. She put the oatmeal box down and then the book. Susan looked down at it and just stopped for a moment, staring at it. Then she looked at Rosie, then back at the book. She looked like she was thinking about something.

"May I?" She reached for the book.

"Sure, Suzy." Rosie decided Susan must really like coloring books. Rosie liked calling a grown-up by her first name. That felt special.

Susan picked up the book. The staple had come out on one end, but it was still all there. Susan was quiet for what seemed like a long time. Rosie saw her swallow once. "Nice coloring book," Susan said, but her voice sounded funny, like she wasn't really talking about the coloring book. "Where did you get it?" Susan looked at Rosie and put the pages down on the porch.

"Thank you. My daddy brought it down from the attic. It's where all the stuff is." Rosie pointed with her thumb towards the house. "It used to belong to a boy named Bobby." Susan blinked. "It says so right in front. See?" Rosie picked up the book and opened it to the first page. "Right here: 'To Bobby From Aunt Zuzu.'" Rosie pointed out the words. "Isn't that a funny name? Aunt Zuzu?" Susan looked at Rosie and nodded, but she wasn't smiling now. "I don't think Bobby was good at coloring. See?" Rosie turned the page to a picture where faded crayon marks were all over the page. Rosie shook her head. "He's not even close to being in the lines." Rosie thought she sounded kind of grown up saying that.

"Yeah, I see," Susan said. "Maybe Bobby was a lot younger than you and didn't really know that well how to color." Susan seemed kind of serious now.

"Well," Rosie nodded in her new grown-up manner, "I can teach him how to do it, if he wants." Now Susan looked like she was going to get sick or something. Her face went all white. Rosie didn't like that.

Susan didn't talk for a minute, then she said, "You said all the stuff is in the attic?" Susan reached for the box of colors, but she wasn't paying attention to which crayon she was getting, and she picked up one that said, "PEACH" on it. Rosie picked out one that was brown, because everyone knows shoes are brown. Well, unless they're black. But Rosie wanted brown shoes.

"Yeah," Rosie nodded. "Mommy said throw it out, it was just junk, but Daddy said keep it, just in case." She focused on the crinkled shoes the elf was making.

"Junk?" Susan began coloring on the shoemaker's sleeping face. Okay, that made sense. His face would be peach colored.

"Yeah, just stuff that was here. Daddy put it all in the attic." Rosie colored carefully, but she got out of the line on one side. Still, it was way better than Bobby had done.

Now Susan was smiling a big smile, and she was coloring in very straight lines across the face of the sleeping shoemaker. "That is a very interesting story, Rosie. Very interesting indeed." She colored some more and seemed happy again and that made Rosie happy.

Chapter 15

Robert pressed down the parking brake and climbed out of the truck near where he had parked it before, leaving the door open. The day had grown warm. An electronic bell sound rang over and over, reminding him his door was open. He walked around and picked up the remnants of his and Susan's lunch. Ants had found the fries already. He shook off the bugs, put it all back in the bag, and wadded the entire mess up. He put it behind the seat of his truck to toss later and gave himself a mild warning to not forget it was there, or his truck would end up reeking in a week's time or less.

He closed the door and walked towards the house, his house, his house that intruders were trying to steal from him. There was Susan, sitting on the porch, her legs folded to one side while she leaned over a page and colored. Her ponytail swayed back and forth slightly as she rubbed the crayon across the little book. The little girl, Rose, was seated across from her, cross-legged, coloring the other page that was open, which meant one of them was coloring an upside-down picture. Well, of course, that would be Susan, he knew. She would do that because Rose would probably have trouble adjusting to that perspective, although, as long as one stays between the lines, it really shouldn't matter much, the way Robert saw it.

He stopped at the edge of the road to watch a second. Susan was engrossed in the coloring and looked to be quite serious about it. Her lips were pursed in concentration, as she had done since childhood. The scene reminded Robert of a long, long time ago, on this very porch, how she had colored in a book with his son, letting him scribble to his heart's desire. Robert stood and let himself enjoy the scene.

He decided he did not want to interrupt the coloring session just yet, so he walked back over to the side of the yard where Luke had been bitten. He made his way around the edge of the garden to where he had picked up Luke earlier. He scanned the ground carefully. If there was a hole somewhere, it might mean there was a den the snake had come out of. If so, it was a much bigger problem than just the one snake.

When he and Bobby lived there, they made sure to keep the yard as clear of chipmunks and field mice as they could. Durn snakes loved to eat them, he thought, then move into their burrows and make families. He and Bobby grew marigolds along the edge of the garden, along with spikes of St. George's Sword, which made their garden look like a curious mixture of flowers and tropical-looking greenery, but they were measures his family had used for years to thwart all manner of vermin. He learned it from his father, who learned it from his. Maybe the measures worked; maybe they didn't. But as long as they saw no snakes, that was all that mattered. And there was also the feeling of at least they were doing something to keep the pests away.

Robert paced along the edge of the yard. There really weren't any holes around that he could see, and he had a practiced eye for such things. The sun above him was tipping towards the southwest, which meant that area of the yard was in the sun. He had a good view. No snakes, no dens. He traced the edges of the yard with his eyes as he strode the area where yard became forest.

In the backyard, two doves fluttered to the ground and began swaggering around, looking for seeds. Then he caught the glint of sunlight from Luke's knife still resting on the ground where he had dropped it in his battle against the viper. That he had lost the battle did not deter the fact that the boy had been brave to fight the beast. Fool-hardy, yes, of course, but still, he surely knew the snake might bite him. It was a brave act done to protect his sister. Robert understood that emotion.

Robert looked back up at the porch and saw both Susan and Rose watching him. He gave a small nod to acknowledge them, then, after checking his surroundings for more would-be attackers, leaned over and picked up the pocketknife. He turned it around in his hand. It wasn't a bad knife. It wasn't a great knife, but he had seen worse. He had certainly used worse knives. It needed cleaning and a good deal of sharpening. He folded and unfolded it. It was a bit hard to open, but clearly Luke had been able to maneuver it.

Now Susan and Rose were walking towards him. They held hands as they walked and that too brought back a memory of his sister with her own girls. Rose looked around her with wide eyes as they grew closer. They made the detour around the edge of the garden, Rose walking very tentatively.

"Don't worry," Robert said. "No more snakes." As he looked down at her, he realized he was smiling. Somewhere inside himself, he had decided before to not be even a little welcoming to these interlopers in his home. Well, he thought now, no harm in smiling at the girl. She wasn't the one who orchestrated this whole squatting ordeal. If anything, she was also a victim of her parents' poor decision-making. Now she was going to be displaced through no wrongdoing of her own.

She looked up at him now and gave him a bright grin. Her hair was pulled back in what was once a ponytail but was leaking out from around the elastic band. "I guess that snake was sure surprised when he found out he could fly, right, Mr. Younger?" Robert held back a laugh, but he could not stop the grin from spreading across his face. Susan laughed.

"I'll bet he was," said Robert. "He won't come back."

"I wouldn't either, if someone very tall threw me into the woods." Rose stood there, holding Susan's hand. Robert shook his head. The girl was certainly precocious.

Susan shook her head in appreciation. "You should see her

do a mourning dove impersonation," she said.

Robert smirked at his sister. "Susan, you can't impersonate a bird. You can only impersonate a person. I'm surprised at you."

Susan released Rose's hand to swat playfully at Robert. "Oh no, not you too?" she said. "One of us is enough in one family."

Rose looked back and forth at the two of them, a curious expression on her face. "But I can do a dove. Want to see, Mr. Younger?"

Robert cocked his head to one side, then stooped down, although he was still much taller than the girl even when he was squatting. "Okay." Rose took on her role as a dove and Robert had to chuckle. "You know what, Rose? That just may be the best dove impersonation I've ever seen." He nodded and glanced up at his sister, since he had deliberately used the same term. "You'd better be careful." He waved with one hand towards the backyard. "Those two birds out back? They might think you belong to them and take you off to their nest." Robert stood and reflexively looked past the house towards where he had seen the two birds earlier.

Rose gave out a giggle. "I wouldn't fit in a nest, would I, Suzy Two?" She looked up at Susan and grinned.

Susan laughed again. "No, you would not." Robert processed what that might be about – Suzy Two?

As Robert watched, the two doves flapped up out of the yard towards the pine tree. "Look," Rose pointed. "They always like that tree, for some reason."

Robert regarded the girl now. "That's where they live, in pine trees. That's probably where their nest is."

"Oh," Rose moved her eyes back and forth from Robert to the pine tree.

"I told you," said Susan. "My brother knows an awfully lot about wild things."

Rose stared up at Robert now. "What are you going to do with Lukie's knife, Mr. Younger?"

Robert had nearly forgotten he was holding it. "Oh." He looked at the little knife in his hand now, folded up. "I don't know. What should we do with it?"

"Well, we could put it back in his hidey-hole," Rose offered. "I know where it is." She said the last part as if it were a deep secret.

"Oh?" Susan asked.

"Yeah, it's behind a board on the other side of the tool shed. Want to see it? He has lots of fun things in there."

"Does he now?" Robert had an image from long ago drift into his mind's eye. How many times had he seen Bobby slink off behind the shed to squirrel away some treasure? He knew exactly where this hiding place was.

"Yeah, he has marbles, and rubber bands, and some pennies, and . . ." Rose paused as she counted on her fingers.

"A slingshot?"

"Yeah," Rose looked up, surprised. "How did you know?"

"Lucky guess." Robert felt a pang from the memory stab softly into his soul. But there was also a sense of closure in it all, that some new boy was now able to enjoy that feeling of having his own gathering of treasures. Boys were like blue jays, attracted to shiny things they then placed in their nests, or, in this case, a secret hiding spot.

"Want to see it?" Rose asked again. She was nearly hopping up and down with excitement.

"No, I know where it is. That has been a hidey-hole for young men for many years. It's Luke's right now. Maybe we should respect that." Robert felt a sigh from deep within him coming out. He braced himself for it. He looked at Rose. "At least for now, okay?" He glanced over and Susan was eyeing him carefully, measuring him, it seemed.

"Okay." Rose was disappointed, but only for a moment. "Hey, want to see our garden, Mr. Younger?"

"Yes. Yes, I'd like that very much." In fact, moving his attention to something new felt like an excellent notion. Robert turned to walk towards the garden, and Rose reached up and put her hand in his. Robert felt himself startled somewhere deep inside. He took her hand and noticed Susan, holding Rose's other hand, looking straight ahead, and grinning from ear to ear.

"Daddy says we will have lots of tomatoes this year." Rose led them along the edge of the neatly tilled rows. "I like tomatoes. Lukie, he doesn't like them much. Those are zucchini plants there." She let go of Robert's hand to point at the small plants already showing signs of taking root.

"That's a lot of zucchini," Susan said. "Six plants?"

"Yeah, that's what Mommy said. She says two squash plants are enough for a neighborhood, but Daddy said they came six to a box." She kept walking. "These are going to be green beans. I love green beans. Mommy puts them in jars, and we eat them all year." The little girl was enjoying being the tour guide. "And those little hills there? That's corn. Lukie loves corn on the cob. Me too." Robert surveyed the plot. They had planted a huge garden. He was glad the mother canned the extra. It would be a pity to waste so much food. He had known hunger, and he never wanted to feel that again for himself, nor anyone else.

"So," Susan interrupted the tour. Robert was glad. He knew, of course, what most of the plants were immediately from sight, and he really wasn't interested in a plant-by-plant description. "Tell me, Rosie. What didn't you plant?"

Rose stopped walking and turned to face Susan. She looked thoughtful for a moment. "Flowers. I wish I could plant some flowers, but Daddy says we got plenty of flowers and we can't eat flowers."

"Actually, you can." Robert looked across the yard. He raised his arm and pointed at the nearly blooming tiger lilies across the road from the house. "See those flowers over there?" Rose followed with her eyes in the direction of the blooms. "Those are delicious. I've eaten lots of them." He pivoted towards the back yard and pointed again. "Those yellow ones back there?"

"Those are dandelions," Rose said.

"Yes, and you can eat not only the flower, but the leaves and even the roots."

"Really?"

"Really."

"Maybe Daddy will let me plant some in the garden." Rose looked up at Robert.

"Well, they are pretty good at planting themselves."

"Oh." Rose frowned.

"What you should plant are marigolds." Robert squatted down again to talk with Rose, resting one arm on his right knee, which was now almost chin level.

"Marigolds?" Rose asked, but she said it as "Mary Golds." Susan glanced suspiciously over at Robert.

"Yes, they are quite tasty, plus . . ." He paused and looked at Susan. "They look very pretty too." No, he was not going to mention snakes to the little girl. He wondered if Susan really thought he was that cold-hearted.

"Look!" Rose pointed at the road where the Jeters' tan car was wending its way towards them. It pulled into the driveway and stopped, and the father climbed out. Robert felt himself tighten all over.

He pulled into the drive like he owned the place. There was a very real part of Robert that wanted to end this right here, right now, and by whatever means necessary. But, there was the little girl running over to her father now, and her brother was in the hospital with a snake bite and, since she was not in the car, he assumed the mother had stayed with the boy, which made sense. It wasn't the right time.

Still, his pulse quickened. Seeing Jeter drive up to the place as if it were his made Robert angry all over again. But, he had promised both Martin and Susan he would do this the "civil" way, although he noted they had wars they called "civil" that were anything but, so maybe the term didn't mean what they thought it did.

Robert followed Susan over towards the house. Terry picked up Rose and stopped on the paver sidewalk to talk with them. "Thanks for watching Rosie." Jeter nodded. "She talk your ear off?"

"No, she was a perfect lady," Susan said. She stood in front of Robert, between the two men, as if she half-expected Robert to sucker punch the man with his child in his arms. Robert wondered just how bad a reputation he had before. He didn't much care for being seen in that light. He wanted to believe he had at least learned better self-control in the last six years.

Then he saw the coloring book lying open on the porch floor and he felt his face flush. He took a half step forward to pick it up, but Susan turned to him. She looked up in his face and widened her eyes. Robert understood what she was saying from that expression. She was saying, "No, not here. Wait. I will tell you more in a little while." Robert let himself be stopped.

"Well, she's a good girl," Jeter lifted her up once in a quick bob on his arm.

Robert made himself calm down. This was how he was now, he decided, able to control his temper and able to be composed. "How's Luke?"

"He's going to be okay. He'll be in the hospital a couple of days, but he's going to be okay." He looked at Robert more seriously now. "Thank you. You saved my boy's life." He reached his hand out from under Rose, still supporting her with his upper arm, and extended it to Robert. Robert took his hand, and they shook. Terry stared up into Robert's eyes. Robert was very glad he had not started some confrontation. Terry pulled his hand back to support Rose. "Wife's gonna stay with him. I need to take her some things." Now he bounced Rose again. "You want to go see Lukie?" he asked the girl.

"Yes, Daddy. Lukie saved me from the snake."

Then Jeter glanced down at Robert's other hand. "Is that the knife Luke was using to try and kill that snake?"

Robert again had forgotten the small blade was in his hand. "Oh, yeah. Here." He reached it out and handed it to Terry.

"Need to throw this out right now," Jeter said half under his breath, putting the girl down on her feet, on the porch next to him.

Robert shrugged. "You could. He's your boy. Do what you see fit. But it's an okay knife. It might be a good chance to teach him how to use it, to take care of it, be safe with it. Needs to learn some time."

Jeter looked back up at Robert. "Yeah, maybe so. Maybe so." Robert turned and Susan turned with him, and they walked towards the truck. He heard the screen door of his house slam shut behind him.

Chapter 16

Susan hurried from room to room, picking up stacks of unfiled bills and receipts from the table and taking them into the family room in the back of the house, sometimes to then take them back into the dining room, when she began straightening the back room. That always bothered her about herself, how she seemed to get in a whirlwind, on the one hand very busy, but more often than not, spinning in circles. She liked to think she was multitasking, but these days, she seemed to be wasting effort, cleaning the bathroom sink, then taking the towels and starting a load of laundry, then noticing the lint on the rug outside the little laundry room and pulling out the vacuum, then feeling the need to move the chairs and the end tables to clean the carpet beneath, but then seeing the stack of unopened mail on the small table next to her reading chair.

Meanwhile, the bathroom was still not finished. At first, Robert leaned against the arched doorway leading into the dining area and watched with a kind of bemused smirk on his face until she upbraided him to get off his lazy butt and help her clean. He looked sufficiently chastised, but his help was almost more trouble than it was worth, since he didn't know where anything went, or, perhaps more honestly, she had yet to decide where everything went.

Finally, when she had cleared most of the clutter from the living room and dining area, she put him onto vacuuming, which she figured he would be fine at, although he looked fairly absurd from the start, his long, lean body curved over the machine so he could hold it down onto the floor. But at least he was helping. Of a sort.

When Susan, busy threading marinated artichoke hearts, olives, and pepperoni onto long bamboo skewers, looked back over at Robert, he was barely moving the nozzle on the vacuum. He kept gazing at the floor, unfocused. His feet were stationary. "Hey," she called over the whine of the suction. He looked up at her. "You have to move it around," she swirled her hand around to get the point across.

"Yeah, yeah." Robert nodded, and he did start pushing and pulling the hose again, but he was still clearly not feeling it. Susan let the thought pass through her mind that someone who has lived in a lean-to made of sticks and leaves somewhere in the middle of the forest probably doesn't take a lot of stock in cleaning floors, but she let it evaporate without saying it.

Besides, Susan had party food to fix. She already had the store-bought meat balls bubbling in the crockpot with a mixture of brown sugar and bourbon. The aroma filled the house: sweet, savory, and slightly boozy. When she finished the antipasto kabobs, she would make the tortilla pinwheels with cream cheese and ham. Yes, they were old-fashioned hors d'oeuvres, but it was what her daughters loved, or so it seemed to her.

What was exciting was, they were on their way home to see their uncle and their Mama too, of course, but Susan would not begrudge them wanting to see Robert after his long absence. Plus, she wanted to make it festive, fun. She loved it when Cassie and Cleo came home. She always wanted it to be celebratory. There was in her thoughts perhaps a worry they might grow tired of returning to Wyler's Ford, of coming home, so maybe if she always made it fun, that wouldn't happen. She didn't worry they would stop loving her, only that they would see their hometown as a place best seen in the rearview mirror. Not that she would blame them; there wasn't much to hold young people in Wyler's Ford, especially once they had been just about any place else.

But they had been very excited when she had texted them their uncle had returned from the wilds. They couldn't wait to come visit. He had been an important part of their lives when they were young, from taking them fishing and hiking. to occasionally having a tea party in the backyard with the girls and their menagerie of dolls and stuffed animals. She could see him in her mind's eye, picking up the tiny teacup of water, his pinkie finger extended, having mock small talk with the Sally Sweetheart doll and Dougie Dog, who were propped up on small pillows taken from the living room couch.

Now she carried an oblong galvanized bucket full of wine spritzers and icy water into the dining room and placed it on a woven rattan placemat. She looked into the living room and Robert was hunched over the machine, moving the nozzle over the same small patch on the rag rug. He was clearly someplace else in his head.

"That's good!" she yelled. The machine stopped howling, and for that she was not sorry. Robert looked at her, his expression blank, his eyes almost glassy. "Go get cleaned up, Robert."

He blinked himself back into the present. "Jeez, Suzy, I just had a shower yesterday." Susan paused. She couldn't quite decide if he was serious. "I thought I might take a walk." He walked over to the wall and unplugged the vacuum.

She decided he was in fact serious about skipping a shower. His nieces were coming to see him; he did not need to be The Goatman when they arrived. She stopped and put her hands on her hips. "No, Robert." Susan shook her head. "No running away. These are your nieces. They love you. Please go get a shower."

He looked at her for just a moment, and Susan could almost see him bolting out the door like a claustrophobic puppy jumping out an exit opened by an unsuspecting guest. "Okay," he said and slumped back towards the bathroom, leaving the vacuum in the middle of the floor.

"And don't use all the hot water. I need to grab a shower too." Susan pulled the vacuum back into the pantry then headed towards the kitchen to pour some mixed nuts into the three-footed bowl that had been their mother's.

"I'm supposed to use hot water?" he called from the hallway. "Well, that changes everything."

She was glad to hear him joking. It meant he was willing himself to calm down. But she knew what was happening. There had been one reunion after another, no matter where they went, and she could see he was tired of being the oddity, the subject of "welcome homes," sometimes well-meaning, sometimes couched in tones that bordered on sarcasm. Susan heard the shower turn on while she worked on her surprise dish.

Susan's hair was still damp, but she at least had her face on when Cassie's coupe pulled next to the curb in front of the house. Cassie and Cleo climbed out and walked up the sidewalk, laughing over some shared joke. They each carried small overnight bags, the very ones Susan had bought for them when they moved out. It was a gift she hoped said, "Go out and explore the world, but be sure you come home occasionally as well." Susan watched them from the window, then looked over at Robert, who was standing by the dining table, eyeing the spread of food.

"Hold off, Robert." She couldn't suppress her own happiness at his return, how glad she was her brother had finally come home. "You might want to answer the door. I think it's for you," she said, just as Cleo opened the door, adjusting the little suitcase from one hand to the other, then, seeing her uncle, simply dropping the case to the floor completely with a clatter and walking quickly across the room to hug him.

He barely had time to turn around before Cleo wrapped her arms around his back with an embrace. Cassie followed her sister, tossing her case onto Susan's reading chair as she passed. It occurred to Susan her daughters might only use those overnight bags when they came home, a kind of thoughtful gesture combined with a sisterly inside joke. But that wouldn't matter to her. No, not one bit.

Now Robert was swarmed by his nieces who were both speaking at once, saying, "Uncle Robert, welcome home!" "We missed you so much!" "You look wonderful, Uncle Robert." "We are so glad to see you." Their voices were similar enough, even Susan could not readily discern which daughter spoke which sentences, but that surely didn't matter. Both of them were expressing the same love, the same relief, the same welcome.

"Thank you," Robert managed to squeeze between exultations. "Thank you. I missed you too. I love you too." He tried to respond to the various comments, but that, of course, was impossible and, to Susan's mind, unnecessary.

"Cassie," Susan interrupted the hugs. "Cleo." She stood for just a moment, waiting for her own welcome, but quickly dismissed her somewhat prideful need. This was about Robert. She knew that. "Let Robert breathe." Her daughters loosened their grips on Robert and smiled adoringly up at him.

"Okay, Mama," Cleo said. "It's just so good to see him again." She glanced at Susan, then back up at Robert, her expression almost one of disbelief.

"I know. Believe me, I know." Susan reached over and picked up Cassie's bag and placed it on the floor next to the arch that led into the dining room.

"I'll bet, Mama," Cassie stood on the other side of Robert He had an arm around each of their shoulders. He stood between them, a warm, tender smile on his face, looking from one to the other and back again. No, Susan decided, he wouldn't run away again now, at least not today. If she would allow herself to admit it, she half-expected him to disappear nearly every day. That he had the Jeters to deal with and did not have access to his home surely did not help.

"Have a spritzer?" Susan picked up two bottles for her daughters and handed them over, then picked up two more while they twisted off the tops. She handed a bottle to Robert who had to lift an arm over Cassie's head to take it from her. Robert took the bottle and looked at it as if he were studying it.

Susan chose them because, first of all, Cleo wasn't actually legal age yet, so she didn't want anything too out of bounds, as she saw it. Plus, they weren't very strong, and then Susan herself rather liked the taste of some of the coolers, as long as they weren't too sweet. She realized Robert hadn't had a drink for six years, from what he had told her, so even the small amount of alcohol in these beverages might taste strong to him. She twisted the top off her own and took a sip. She liked the underlying sangria taste, but it sure was sweet. She watched Robert open his and take a swig and, from his grimace, it was clearly a bit sweet for him. "Come on, sit down, everyone. Let's just relax."

"We've been sitting for an hour," Cassie noted, her eyebrows raised. Susan only gave her a smile and sat herself in her reading chair by the window. Her daughters took their cue and went to sit on the couch. Robert placed the bottle he held onto the small table in a motion that said, "I think I'm done with that," then leaned back into the wingback.

Cassie and Cleo asked the same questions everyone did, at least at first. "Where did you go? Are you glad to be back? Meet anyone interesting?" And Robert answered them patiently, although some of his responses Susan had heard often enough to hear they were nearly practiced replies. But Susan understood. The facts of his journey were the same, whenever anyone asked. The response wasn't likely to change. When the conversation lagged just a bit, a gap between getting re-acquainted and returning to normal, Susan stood and turned towards the dining table.

"Well, I have some snacks for us." She walked past the table and into the kitchen. She glanced back at her daughters, who were looking at each other and smiling, nonverbal sister-speak taking place between them. Susan decided the old-fashioned hors d'oeuvres were perhaps less their favorites and more the source of patronage of their mother. She raised an eyebrow. She had suspected this, and now seeing them suppressing grins confirmed it.

She opened the fridge and pulled out the tray she had prepared. She carried it to the table and put it on a different pad. Cassie and Cleo cocked their heads, then looked at each other in a bit of shock. Susan liked that she had surprised them.

"Okay, the way you do this is, you take a piece of the butter lettuce, put some corned beef in the middle, toss on a couple chunks of red onion, put a little brown mustard on it, then squeeze the lime on it. You'll like it."

She couldn't help beaming a tad. Cleo gave her mother a sidelong glance that Susan took as approval and helped herself to the food. Susan let everyone else go first, then put together her own plate and retrieved a bamboo tray to put the plate on. Susan had never liked the idea of folks having to balance plates on their laps. She always had trays. Yes, maybe the other dishes were tried and true, and maybe it was she herself who liked them, but the lettuce cups were even better than she had hoped. Or maybe they were just different.

Everyone sat in the spots they had sat in before, as if having chosen that particular place was a kind of commitment, their trays on their knees, munching happily. After a few minutes, and several appreciated compliments of the fare, Cleo put her tray atop the ottoman before the couch and took a drink from the wine cooler. Unless Susan misread her reaction, it was perhaps a bit sweet for Cleo's taste as well.

"Uncle Robert," she started, in what seemed almost rehearsed tones. "What are you going to do now that you're back?" She put the bottle back onto her tray and sat back, her hands folded around one knee that she propped up now on the edge of the ottoman.

Robert looked up. He had a fold of lettuce, carefully filled and perched atop three fingers, but he stopped and put it back onto his paper plate. "Well, Cleo, that's something I've been pondering myself."

"You are staying, right?" Cassie chimed in.

Robert nodded. "Yeah, yeah, I am, but I'm still trying to figure out just what that means."

"What that means?" Cassie and Cleo said in unison.

Robert put his tray on the little table next to the wingback and leaned forward. He watched his thumbs as he rubbed his hands together. "I spend a lot of time wandering around these days," he said.

"And playing your flute," Susan added.

"Recorder, but yeah," Robert corrected.

"Play a song for us?" Cassie slid her tray atop Cleo's, stacking the two plates.

"Dear God, if I hear 'We Three Kings' one more time, my head may explode." Susan rolled her eyes.

Robert gave a chuckle. "No, not right now, Cassie."

"Are you going to go back to cabinet making? Carpentry?" Cleo asked. "You always loved making things."

"I did, do, did," Robert fumbled over his time reference, as if unsure of it himself.

"I still have the covered box you made for me that Christmas," Cassie smiled.

"I have mine too," Cleo added.

"Yeah, I did love making those." Robert nodded.

"It was part of who you were, Uncle Robert."

Robert looked over his hands at Cleo, seemingly processing that comment.

"Remember the dollhouse, Cleo?" Cassie's eyes lit up with the memory.

"I do. Best . . .present . . .ever." Cleo paused between the words for emphasis. "You could make those and sell them, Uncle Robert."

"Huh," Robert blinked. "Yeah, I don't know. I could. I kind of walked off and left all my tools though. Guess I'd have to start over."

"Maybe," Susan stood to clear the trays. She wished Robert could have enjoyed that last bite. She left his and picked up her own and her daughters' trays. He might come back to it. Cassie moved to stand, but Susan simply laid a hand on her shoulder to say, "Thank you. I've got this."

"You remember 'The Elves and the Shoemaker?'" Susan said, balancing the trays. Cassie and Cleo looked up quizzically, but Robert's expression was more one of intrigue.

"Yeah?" he said.

"Seems the Jeters kept your stuff in the attic." Susan turned and left the room with the trays.

"Wait," Robert stood. "My tools are in the attic?" He rose now and followed Susan as far as the doorway.

"Who are the Jeters?" Cleo asked from the living room.

"The squatters," Cassie reminded her.

"Oh, yeah."

"I don't know what's in the attic exactly, of course, but they kept some stuff, obviously."

"That would be great if you still had your tools, Uncle Robert." Now Cassie was standing next to Robert, and both of them watched Susan toss the plates and drop the utensils into the sink.

"Yeah," Robert looked a little stunned and stared towards the stream of sunlight coming through the kitchen window. "Maybe. Maybe." Susan marched back into the living room and took her seat in her reading chair. She picked up her wine and took a sip. It tasted for all the world like pancake syrup, with the faint whang of alcohol in it.

"I'm sorry, but this stuff is terrible." She stood now and picked up her bottle and began gathering the others. "Anyone want a beer?"

"Yes," all three of them said in unison. Susan smiled at her mistake. Wine coolers. Who was she trying to kid?

She brought back four bottles of beer. She didn't bring glasses. Her finger-food party was now just family, talking, having a beer, and losing the pretense. "I don't know," she said, handing out the bottles. "That tool shed looks like it hasn't been touched much. Looks like they keep gardening stuff inside, but not sure what else."

Robert leaned familiarly over the back of the wingback, both hands holding the beer in front of him. "Well, well," he started. "Power tools would probably be shot. Too old now anyway, I imagine." It wasn't lost on Susan how his train of thought had turned to the condition of his tools. Purpose. That's what her brother needed. He needed to find himself a new purpose. Or even his old one, if that's what he wanted. Robert straightened, took a long swig of the cold, bitter beer, then came around and sat again. "I don't know. Been a long time." He looked over at Cassie and Cleo and focused again on them. They returned gentle smiles to their uncle.

"If you don't go back to carpentry, how will you make a living?" Now Cleo took a drink in a move that made clear to Susan this was far from her first beer.

"Well, turns out I have some money." Robert held up his beer in a kind of airy toast.

"Yeah," Cassie said, looking down at her beer.

"Yeah," echoed Cleo. These two could no more play poker than they could play hopscotch on an ice rink, Susan thought. Yes, she had told them about Robert's money, but they might have acted a little, what, surprised, or happy? Susan shook her head, then took another sip of beer. It was so much better than that god-awful cooler she had bought. It's perhaps what she got for trying to put on airs.

Susan decided all pretense was gone anyway. "You know, Robert. Even as much as you have, it won't last forever. You gotta have an income." There was a part of her that wanted to help her brother at pretty much all costs, and a part that worried he was one buttinsky sister away from hightailing into the wilderness again. Robert looked at her, but Susan couldn't read it. Was he getting edgy? She didn't think so.

Cleo came to her rescue. "My econ professor says your money needs to work for you, not the other way around."

"Is that so?" Robert returned his gaze to his two nieces. He nodded. Again, Susan couldn't read it. The room grew quiet for a moment. Perhaps Susan had overstepped. Robert was a difficult study.

Finally, Cassie broke the silence. "Are you moving out the squatters, Uncle Robert?"

"Yeah," he nodded, and Susan was grateful for the change in subject. "I think so."

"You think so?" Cleo asked. "You're not sure?"

"There's a lot to consider." Robert took another swig from his beer. If he hadn't had a drink in all those years, the beer seemed to be going down easily now. The room grew quiet again. Each of them used sips of beer to fill the awkwardness of the pause.

"Have you been to Memorial Gardens since you got back?" Cassie asked, and Susan nearly spit out the half-drink she had in her mouth. She hadn't mentioned all that yet. Cassie, of course, couldn't know that. "We got a nice marker for Bobby's grave." Robert's eyes opened wide. He was silent and looked for all the world like someone had just hit him as hard as they could in his solar plexus.

"You did?" he finally managed. Then before anyone could answer, he said, "No, not yet," shaking his head slowly.

"Yeah," Cleo said. "We did. Bobby was the best cousin ever. He was a brother to us."

"Walked us from the bus stop every day," Cassie added.

"Yep, and not one boy ever tried anything," Cleo laughed.

"Yeah, well, that wasn't always a good thing." Cassie and Cleo shared a glance and doubled up with laughter.

Susan saw the look on Robert's face, as if he never thought about how they too suffered a great loss when Bobby was killed. Robert gave a wan smile. "He was a good boy, wasn't he?"

"You mean a good man, Uncle Robert." Cleo took another sip of beer. "Bobby was a man in the seventh grade. He had a five-o'clock shadow in middle school."

"He always took care of us," Cassie added.

"Huh," Robert sighed. "He took care of me, too, only I didn't always see that. He took care of everyone."

"Yeah, it was kind of who he was." Susan thought back to all the times her nephew had simply shown up and mowed the lawn or watched the girls while Susan shopped at the Piggly Wiggly.

"You know," Robert said, "I thought he was mine, and when he was taken, I felt it was my loss, my burden to bear, that no one else could possibly feel the way I felt." He nodded.

"Now I know, he was much more than mine. He was much more than ours, even." Robert paused. He looked over at Susan, then back to her daughters. "One day, I was fishing beside a beaver pond, kind of out in the middle of nowhere. There was an old man there, he lived close by, I found out later, and he tossed a stone into the water. I hid, because, well, that's sort of what I did then, but I did watch. And as I watched the ripples of water go across the pond, I realized something. I realized that not only was Bobby ours, we were his, and we all sort of go together, like the different parts of that little beaver pond all fit together." Cassie and Cleo watched their uncle intently. Susan did too, but this was different. This was not running away. "That's when I understood. I thought it was a question of what happens when we go, when any particular wave across that pond stops. Then I realized, we don't stop. We simply return ourselves to the pond that we always were, and that pond is bigger than any one of us and deeper than all of us."

Susan glanced over at Cassie, whose eyes glistened with tears. Robert saw it too and stood, towering over the three of them for just a moment. Then he stepped across the ottoman and sat between Cassie and Cleo and put an arm around each of them. They let themselves be pulled into the group hug, each of them with a hand in his chest. Then Robert laughed, a deep, hearty laugh that was apropos of nothing Susan could discern. Cleo pulled back, curious.

"Susan," Robert said after he caught his breath. "Remember those pictures Pop always liked?" Susan tried to imagine what he was talking about. "Remember, the ones where it's all squiggly lines and you can't tell what it is? Then you get tired of staring at it, and you go wall-eyed, and suddenly you see it. It's a three-dimensional picture of, I don't know, a porpoise or The Taj Mahal or something. Remember?"

"Um, yeah. He had a whole book of them." Susan tried to place the memory.

"Yeah," Cassie said, too excited for the topic, as Susan saw it. "Grandpa loved those. I remember. What were they, Magic

166

Eye?"

"Yeah!" Robert yelled, and he stood suddenly. "Magic Eye. That's it." Susan could not imagine why that recollection made Robert so happy. "It's like staring at a Magic Eye picture. I couldn't see it because of all the little distractions, even though I was looking right at it. Then, once you see it, you wonder why it was so hard to see it in the first place." Robert stepped back over the ottoman and Cassie and Cleo stood now too, as if energized by Robert's sudden burst.

"What are you talking about, Robert?" Susan stood now too, feeling awkward to stay seated when everyone else was standing.

Robert turned and looked at her. He was grinning all over his face. "I'm talking about what comes next. I'm talking about the pond," he yelled. "I'm talking about the Taj Mahal." Then he laughed again. Susan looked over at her daughters, who wore happy smiles, contagion from their uncle, but all they could do was shrug at her and shake their heads in wonderment.

Chapter 17

Robert swung the rack of plants over the tailgate and placed them in the back of the truck, bracing them against the spare tire he had put in the truck bed the night before. Susan, sitting in the passenger seat of the cab with her elbow resting on the window opening, did not turn around. It had rained earlier in the day and the air had a dewy scent here in mid-morning, although the sun peeked in and out of clouds now. Robert climbed behind the wheel and started up the motor.

"You sure about this?" Susan asked as he shifted into gear. "Really sure?"

"Suzy Two, I'm not sure I have ever in my life been as certain of anything." Robert let out the clutch and they pulled through the dirt lot and onto the gravel, dirt, and mud road, passing the hand-lettered sign that read: "Marlene's Greenhouse." Susan smiled at Robert calling her that and he could tell she looked forward to seeing little Rosie again. He did too. She had made an impression on both of them.

"When is Martin supposed to be there?" Susan swayed with the truck as they slowly navigated the rutted drive towards the chip-and-seal county road. Marlene's was where they had bought plants for years. Marlene was the mother of one of Susan's high school pals from years before and had built her greenhouse behind the old homestead long before anyone else much thought about such things. At first, their patronage of

Marlene was simply helping out a friend's mom as she started her business on the side, a kind of profitable avocation, but the truth was, she was very good at producing the starter plants, and now they were the best that could be found in the county.

"Same time as last time you asked, Suzy: one o'clock." The turn signal blinked loudly as they made their way back towards town.

"Yeah, okay. It is just such a big decision." Susan rocked loosely back and forth with the movement of the truck as it climbed onto the county road, letting the motion go through her rather than stiffening up against it, which only made it worse. "And where will you go?" Robert heard the real question: Are you running off again? "You can stay with me as long as you want, you know." The ride smoothed out now on the county lane.

"I know. And thanks for that. I'm afraid I'm cramping your love life though, Sis. But it'll work out. You'll see." Robert rested his left hand on the steering wheel, his right hand on the gear shift. It felt good to be behind the wheel again.

"Right," Susan laughed. "As if." She paused. "And the Jeters' guy is going to be there too? What's his name?"

"Phil Something-or-other." Robert did a half-shrug with his left hand.

"Yeah, he's gonna be there?"

"Martin said he would be, yes. Would you stop worrying?" Robert glanced over at Susan. She was just trying to take care of him. He appreciated it. Robert saw the side road almost too late. Funny how much closer things were when he drove instead of hiked overland. He clicked the turn signal, took a sudden turn, and headed up a narrow blacktop road.

"Where we going?" Susan lurched back and forth again as he made the turn, perhaps a little fast. "This isn't the way to your house?" Then she caught herself, as if saying that was the wrong thing to say.

"No," now Robert downshifted and headed up the hill. "Need to see a man."

"Robert?" Susan bounced with the turns.

"Patience, sister. Patience." Robert used both hands to steer the truck up the curving road. The transmission gave a high-pitched whine as he headed up the lane, still perhaps a little fast, he realized. He checked the mirror to see how the plants were doing, but they hadn't slid. The tire had kept them stationary.

"Jeez, Robert, you gotta pee or something? Slow down." Susan was so light, she tossed back and forth as he maneuvered the truck. She tried to brace herself against the glove box. He laughed and decided that he should indeed back off the accelerator. In fact, his only hurry was in his energy to see this through, he realized. He had no pressing deadline. The truck stopped weaving so violently when he slowed, and Susan brushed her hair back. "Where the hell . . .?" Then she looked up through the windshield. There was the cell tower next to the pond. "Jimmy's?" Susan looked over at Robert. "We're at Jimmy's," she said, as if he might not realize it.

"Yep, Jimmy's." Robert slowed even more to take the turn towards the Barlow farmhouse and there in the field was Jimmy, bouncing along on his FarmAll, knocking down the weeds. "What do you think, Sis?" Robert nodded towards his pal. "Getting ready to plant Bermuda grass?" Robert stopped the truck when Jimmy saw them and started waving.

"Yeah, likely." Susan raked her hair from her cheek. Robert felt bad for throwing her around so. He had to try and calm down. That was, after all, the whole point of what he had decided. He was just going to calm down and think things through and do things the best way possible, in a way that Bobby might approve, when it came right down to it, although Robert did not intend to live his life as a kind of paean to death. He had taken that route, and he was done with it. No, but he could be mindful just the same.

Jimmy wore a wide grin as he chugged over to where Robert had pulled the truck up and stopped, still very much in the road, but hardly anyone ever came up this way. The chances of someone driving up were low, and besides, there was room to pass. Susan climbed out the passenger side. She slid from the cloth seat to the gravel at the edge of the road. The blacktop still had moist spots, but it was drying quickly.

"Robert. Susan," Jimmy called as he waved with one massive hand, jostling towards them. He pulled up next to the road, the tractor half-turned to make another pass over the field. "How are my favorite Youngers doing?" He turned off the tractor and made a practiced, three-step dismount. He walked towards them with his hand outstretched.

"I'm telling Daddy you said that," teased Susan, walking towards him.

"Uh oh, don't do that." Jimmy laughed as he shook Robert's hand, then Susan's. "What brings you two up to Barlow's Pond? Too cold for swimming." Jimmy grinned and took a step back. He shoved his hands into the back pockets of his denim coveralls. He stood, solid, his legs looking like tree trunks.

Robert rubbed his chin. "I'd like to talk to you about that tract of land you've got down on Hickory Creek." Jimmy's eyes opened wide. "Rumor has it, it's for sale," Robert pretended Jimmy hadn't already told him he was considering selling it.

"Maybe, maybe." Jimmy studied Robert's face. "Depends on the buyer. Can't be letting just anyone move that close to the farm."

"I get that," Robert dropped his hand to his side and shifted his weight to one leg. "Got county water down there?"

"Oh yeah," Jimmy was still trying to figure out the angle. "Every county road has water now. Not bad for our little neck of the woods."

"No, that's good." Robert nodded. He decided to continue this act of indirect interest. "Got electricity?"

"Yeah, it does. Ernie Tisdale has his place just a mile or so up. Power company ran the lines along the road. Be pretty easy to hook up, I reckon." Then Jimmy grew weary of the game. He leaned forward. "What's this about, Robert? You know someone wants to buy it? I don't want a trailer pulled in back there. I got nothing against trailers, but that's not a good spot there. It's too wooded, too natural. I wouldn't like that." Jimmy shook his head and looked at the tufts of weeds at his feet. His hands were still parked in his back pockets.

"I'm interested, Jimmy." Robert dropped the charade. "It's me. I'd like to buy that piece of land from you and build myself a house there."

"What?" Jimmy and Susan said at the same time.

"You got a house, Robert," Jimmy protested. His eyebrows were furrowed in confusion.

"Decided I'm going to rent it out," Robert said. Susan nodded. She knew that part. "I want to build my own place. That house over on Willow? That was my Grandpa's. Okay for what it was, and I made some changes and all, but I have some ideas about how I'd like to build a place." Robert nodded at his friend, then at Susan, who stood staring at him.

"Not using sticks and tarps and such, right?" Susan asked, and Robert got the distinct feeling she was only half-joking.

"Well, stick built, yes, but, no, a traditional kind of place. But with some tricks I may have picked up along the way."

"Oh?" Jimmy asked.

"Yeah, like a way I thought of for doing a fireplace that would get more heat out of the wood and draw better. And I'd like to do separate drainage systems, one for grey water that I can recycle, one for black water."

'Huh," Jimmy snorted.

"You're just chock full of surprises these days, aren't you, Robert?" Susan crossed her arms now and looked at him, shaking her head, but Robert saw no disapproval, simply surprise.

"Sometimes, if I try hard enough, I surprise myself." Robert gave her a smile.

"No doubt." Susan unfolded her arms, reached over, and patted Robert's shoulder.

"Hells bells, Robert." Jimmy took the step towards Robert, removed his hands from his pockets, and wrapped his arms around Robert. He had moved so quickly, Robert's arms were pinned to his sides. Then Jimmy gave his usual bear hug, lifting

Robert off his feet.

"Hey, put me down, Jimmy." Robert squirmed. Jimmy let him down and stepped back to look up into Robert's face.

"Robert, I will give you that land. I can't think of anything I would rather have than you as a neighbor. We are going to have a blast." Robert saw a glimpse of his old friend, ready to take on dares and getting into minor trouble for the sake of adventure. It was funny, Robert thought, how grown men can retain that boyish taste for misadventure when they get around their old pals.

"Thanks, Jimmy." Robert rubbed his ribs. Jimmy was still incredibly strong. "But I already owe you." Robert turned and waved at the truck. "I'm going to buy the land from you, if you'll sell it to me."

"Well, yeah, sure," Jimmy shrugged. "Like I said, I'd love to have you that close by. I figure it's worth about ten thousand. It's no good as farmland, but that's what I had hoped a hunter might pay."

"No, I won't pay ten thousand," Robert shook his head. Susan turned and looked at him, her eyebrows raised.

Jimmy's eyes opened wide too. "Uh, well, I told you I'd give it to you, Robert." He held his arms up before him in a kind of surrender.

"Jimmy, there's a creek there, a nice pool where it oxbows, and there's always game and fish there. There's a riffle just above that with smallmouth in it. The timber is mature, a nice mix of hardwoods, some pine trees. The place is full of everything I want, Jimmy. I won't pay less than twenty for it. That's my final offer." Robert waved his hands in a "safe" motion.

Now Susan lowered her face and looked up at Robert. Jimmy's jaw dropped.

"You drive a hard bargain, Robert, but you win," Jimmy grinned. Robert knew the money was going to help, a lot. Was he giving away his money, he wondered. Perhaps he was. But he had discovered just how little he could get by on, and if he could help out his friend who had been steadfast through it all, he couldn't think of a better use for the money. And he was certain Bobby would agree.

"Okay then. Done and done."

"Done and done," echoed Jimmy, still smiling, his eyes bright.

"I'll have Martin Douglas draw up the papers, Jimmy."

"Okay." Jimmy stood there, nodding his head.

"Those weeds won't knock themselves down," Susan pointed at the half-mowed field. Jimmy turned and walked back towards the tractor without saying more. Robert could almost see the thoughts spinning around in his friend's head. Susan turned and looked up at Robert. "You sure know how to spice things up, big brother." She started for the truck. "I'm so glad you're back."

"Me too, Sis." Robert walked around the truck bed towards the cab. "Wait 'til you see what I have in mind for your place." He slid in and Susan glanced over at him. He laughed. "Well, I need a place to stay until I at least get the roof up. And I intend to earn my keep." He started up the engine and shifted into gear. "I mean," he said as he let out the clutch, "did you think I was going to live in a tent?"

Chapter 18

Terry worked the garden hoe along the edge of the row of just peeking-out squash plants. There were a few weeds, although not a lot, but he wanted to stay ahead of them. He also broke up the dirt some from where the rain earlier had made it cake down a bit, although it was drying now. Each time he turned a piece of the earth, the scent of copper and moss rose up to him. He liked the smell.

Rose followed behind him, occasionally shifting the galvanized metal bucket to pick up and throw in the weeds he dislodged. She was a surprisingly good helper to be as young as she was, better even than Luke. But that wasn't fair.

Terry paused in his chopping of the clods to look up at the porch where Luke sat in the old rocker, covered in a quilt. He was mending, but he was nowhere near back to his old self. Luke looked back at his father, but his expression didn't change. That was the real difference. The boy had zero energy. He looked out at Terry and Rose working in the garden and barely registered even seeing what was taking place. Now Charlene came out the front door with a cup that she handed to Luke. Terry saw him slowly turn his gaze towards his mother and shake his head, but Charlene spoke to him, nodding her head, and Terry saw Luke's hand reach out from under the quilt and take the cup.

It had to be canned chicken noodle soup. It was Charlene's cure for pretty much every ailment. But that was okay. Terry liked canned soup well enough, perhaps because he rarely had homemade soup, and now Luke was raising the cup to his mouth. That was good. The doctors said it would take maybe a couple of weeks for him to get better. At least he was eating. Before, that had never been a problem for Luke. Although he was as thin as wet rope with a ten-pound weight on it, the kid could pack it away. Usually, keeping him fed was a major expense for the Jeters. And now that Charlene had to take time off from the day care center to nurse Luke back to health, it was even more of a worry. But, Terry thought, all you can do is all you can do.

"Daddy?" Rose had caught up to him while he was lost in thought. She stood behind him, holding the bucket with the smattering of weeds in it, looking up at him as if to say, "Get a move on."

"Oh, look at you, Rosie. Got all the weeds?" Terry stooped down to speak with his daughter, slanting the handle of the hoe as he lowered himself to his haunches.

"Yes, Daddy." She held up the bucket for him. "See?" Then she put it down and reached into it and pulled out a dandelion seed head. "Look, Daddy, it's a dandy lion."

"Yes, it is," he said, but before he could say anything more, she blew on the seeds and they floated out, picked up the slight breeze, and drifted across the garden. Terry stood and watched them scatter. He felt his body sag a bit at the thought of so many dandelions in the vegetable patch.

"Mr. Younger says we can eat them." Rose watched the seeds glide in a careless, easy spread.

"Does he now?" Terry shook his head and picked up his hoe. "Well, we might have to if they take over the garden." He couldn't be upset with her. Who didn't love blowing on a dandelion head and making a wish? He dropped a corner of the hoe blade next to a small tuft of field brome. He heard the doves behind the house, coo-cooing to each other. He could feel the sweat forming under his shirt. It had been a cool morning, but it was warming now. Besides, Terry Jeter could break into a sweat ice fishing. He had always been that way. He chopped his way along the row.

"Terry?" Charlene called from the porch.

Terry looked up and saw her pointing at the road. He followed the direction of her arm and saw the pickup truck turning around in the road. It was that Younger fellow. This was fine, Terry thought. He didn't have enough to worry about and now, it seemed, everything was about to blow up.

Phil Robinson, their *de facto* attorney, had said he was coming by after lunch, but Terry had no idea it had progressed to this. Would Sheriff Aster be there to escort them away? Phil had said they actually had almost no chance of winning an adverse possession case. Terry put the metal curve of the hoe blade against the ground and leaned his jersey-gloved hands heavily on the handle. He felt suddenly tired.

"Look," Rose called as she sprinted across the garden. She paid no attention to where anything might be growing. "It's Suzy Two and Uncle Robert." She raced across the patch of yard just as the passenger door opened and the Younger woman slid out onto the gravel shoulder of the road.

"Uncle Robert?" Terry glanced around himself, shaking his head, looking for a mooring of some kind.

"Well," Charlene was coming towards him, stepping from the tightly mowed lawn into the garden. She focused on the rows and stepped gingerly over the just-sprouted radishes. "He does remind me of your Uncle Pete a little."

"Does he now?" Terry shook his head to make some sense of things. "Uncle Pete should be getting released in another month or two." He raised his eyebrows at Charlene.

"Oh, you," she mock-scolded him. "You know what I mean. He's tall." She turned, and Terry and Charlene saw the Youngers, now sitting up on the lowered tailgate, perhaps eating lunch. Yes, it was lunch. They pulled wrapped sandwiches from a bag.

Now Rose had reached them, and "Uncle Robert' picked her up and sat her between him and his sister. Terry considered whether or not to call Rose back, but the man had pretty much saved Luke's life. Somehow, this Younger guy did not feel like someone who would harm Rose. Would he be so trusting of Uncle Pete, he wondered. Probably not. No, his dispute with Younger was a legal one, nothing more. And, Terry supposed, today is when it would come to a head. He wondered if Rose would still want to call him "Uncle" once he had thrown them out on their butts.

Charlene looked at Terry again, a look that said, "We might as well go over. What more can we lose?" She took a step towards the truck and Terry followed her, the hoe a makeshift walking stick. Charlene noticed the hoe in his hand and turned her head to look at him.

Terry detoured towards the edge of the garden and leaned the hoe against the metal pole that still had two strands of a laundry line strung between it and a maple tree towards the back of the house. She was right. He didn't need to go over with anything that might be construed as a threat, although if it came to blows, Terry would probably need the weapon. The man was at least eight inches taller than he. He made his way over to the truck where Charlene was saying hello awkwardly and Rose was merrily munching on French fries from a plain white bag.

"Look, Daddy," Rose pointed towards the bed of the truck with a fry. "Mary Golds."

Terry stopped at the side of the truck. There was indeed a whole flat of marigolds, pushed back into the bed of the truck next to an old tire. "So I see," he said. He looked at Robert.

"If you don't mind, I thought we might plant them along the outer edge of the garden," Robert said between bites of a hamburger. It reminded Terry that he himself was about ready for some lunch.

"Edge of the garden," Terry repeated, trying to fathom the intent.

"Hey Rosie?" Susan said now, looking at Terry's daughter. "Think maybe Luke would like a French fry?"

Rose's eyes brightened and she squirmed towards the back of the tailgate she was perched on. "Yeah, Lukie loves French fries." Charlene helped her down, and Susan handed Rose a small white sack half-full of fried potatoes. Rose took off at a gallop.

"Don't spill them," Susan called after her, and Rose did slow down and watched her hand as she trotted up the pavers towards the front porch where Luke sat glumly. When he saw what Rose had, Luke did manage a wan smile.

"'Mary Golds' will help keep out the snakes," Robert said, emphasizing the little girl's pronunciation. He nodded and took another bite of sandwich. "As well as gophers and mosquitoes, and all sort of nasty critters," he said with his mouth full.

"Is that so?" Terry rubbed his chin. Who were these flowers for, he wondered. If the Youngers were displacing the Jeters, it wasn't like Terry had a lot of choice in the matter. These two could steal their garden and plant anything they wanted.

"Yeah," Robert nodded. He took a slurp through a straw of a dark drink. "And they are quite edible."

"Edible?" Charlene scowled. "Eat flowers?" She looked over at Terry, a question all over her face. Terry looked back, but he had no idea how to respond.

"Yeah, Robert eats pretty much everything." Susan wadded up a wrapper and tossed it into the white bag.

"Hey, they're good," Robert protested. "I swear they are." He wadded up his wrapper and put it in the sack as well. Now Rose was running back towards them. Luke was sitting up straighter in the rocking chair, eating fry after fry. As long as he ate, Terry had no complaint.

Robert stood now and the truck bed rose a bit with him. "Got a shovel?" But he took long strides towards the toolshed without waiting for an answer. Now Susan was grappling with the wide plastic box full of flower sets. She scooted it closer to the back of the truck, and Terry picked it up and started for the garden. Charlene looked at him as if he might know what in the world was happening, but all Terry could do was shrug and wag the plants over towards the edge of the garden. Susan crawled crab-like off the truck bed, which did not move when she did.

"Oh boy, oh boy," Rose hopped up and down. "We're

planting flowers in the garden, Mommy." She skipped over towards where Terry put down the flowers and leaned over them. "This one is Mary Gold," she pointed at a small flower. "This one is Mary Red," she looked up at Terry. "See? She has some red in her."

"Are you naming all of them?" Charlene had made her way to the spot with Susan behind her. Susan pulled on some small gardening gloves.

"Maybe," Rose said with her head tilted upwards in a tiny display of contrariness.

"Are you going to able to eat them if they have names?" Susan asked.

Rose giggled. "Suzy, it's not like they're baby ducks or anything." Rose shook her head.

Now Susan gave out a chuckle. "No, I guess not."

Terry looked up to see where Robert had gotten to. The shovel was just inside the door of the shed. It couldn't be that hard. He saw Robert just standing there, looking inside the opened door. Terry walked over and saw what he was looking at. The two doves fluttered from the ground to the pine tree. The air was filled with the faint odor of oil and metal.

There in the shed were hammers hung between ten penny nails, a couple of hand saws hung similarly through holes in the blades. A wooden rack of drill bits was still there from when Terry had first opened the building, as well as a wooden mallet with a leather lanyard, a T-square, and a whole rack of pliers and cutters and wrenches. Mismatched screw drivers rested in a board filled with holes nailed against a support. A level and a tape measure sat on a small shelf. When Terry saw what Robert was looking at, he stopped and noticed them again for the first time in a long time. Terry had kept it in his mind that if times got tough, he could sell them, but mainly, he didn't think about them anymore.

"Sawhorses are still here," Robert waved towards a corner. Terry wondered why in the world that was what he seemed to notice, but then Robert added with a shrug of both hands, "It's all still here."

"Well, I've used some things just to fix stuff around the house." He caught himself up short, wondering how to even talk about the place. "But mostly, I just didn't know how to use a lot of it." Terry shrugged. Robert turned his head and looked at Terry and blinked at him. The two men looked at each other for a moment. "Yeah," Terry said, finally. "You're welcome?" He knew what the man wasn't saying, but it still felt awkward. Now Robert reached in and pulled out two spades and handed one to Terry, who took it in one hand. "Um," Terry fumbled a bit. "Bunch of other stuff in the attic," he motioned with his free thumb over his shoulder. Now Robert let a smile crawl across his face, and he turned, and the two men took their spades and returned to the garden.

"And this one can be Suzy Gold," Rose was pointing at the small sets Susan had laid out along the edge of the garden. Charlene was returning from the house, pulling on some grungy cotton work gloves. Luke was trudging behind her, still wrapped in the quilt, but at least moving. "And this one is Mommy Gold." Rose stooped over each plant and pointed.

"Ten inches apart," Robert Younger turned a spade full of dirt next to the garden.

At least he wasn't digging up the green peppers to plant flowers. The ground was soft from the moisture and the digging went quickly. Luke was put in charge of measuring the distance between sets. Robert and Terry dug the neat, straight line extending the garden by half a foot. Charlene and Susan planted the flowers with trowels. Rose went along the row, naming the plants, talking to each plant, telling them to "Grow up pretty."

Eventually, Terry had her empty the bucket of weeds into the compost pile on the other side of the house and start bringing half-pails of water to slosh onto each plant. They had nearly finished the row when Martin Douglas's SUV pulled up behind the Younger's truck. Martin and Phil Robinson exited out of either side of the car and Martin waved at them. Phil wore khakis and a golf shirt. Martin had on a coat and tie.

Terry was wet all over from perspiring and this felt like a final insult, to have worked on the garden only to be told he had to abandon it to Robert. He felt insulted and angry, but mainly he felt tired, too tired to fight it anymore. Robert looked up at Martin, then shoved his spade into the soil to hold it in place. He turned to Terry.

"Mr. Jeter, Mrs. Jeter, can we talk?" Robert nodded towards Martin and Phil, who seemed to have decided the lowered tailgate of the truck would serve as a boardroom table to evict the Jeters from their home that they had lived in for this past five years. It was the only home Rose knew. Luke loved it here. Charlene had even grown to like it, although at first she had been resistant to moving into someone's house while they were gone. And, now that Terry thought about it, perhaps she had been right. Still, they had saved a pretty good little nest egg. If they would need to move, at least maybe they could afford something decent, which, at the time they had found this little house not being lived in, they could not.

Terry walked behind Robert towards the two lawyers in the road. Charlene fell in beside him as he passed. Rose and Luke watched it all carefully, while Susan, on her knees, troweled the plants into the row.

"Rosie?" Susan looked up.

"Yes, Suzy Two?" Terry heard behind him now.

"We need to get some water for Mary Orange, don't we?"

Terry heard the clank of the metal handle on the pail. He would have put his arm around Charlene as they walked, give her some sense of support, but he was entirely too sweaty for that. But just walking beside her, he could feel the heaviness of her step. The two of them came up to where Martin and Phil were shaking hands and exchanging greetings with Robert. Martin had laid his briefcase flat on the lowered tailgate and opened it. Several manila folders were stacked inside. Now Robert turned to Terry and Charlene as they arrived in the group.

Martin Douglas spoke before anyone else, as if he were in a rush. "Robert, I believe you wanted to talk with the Jeters, with us here?" Robert glanced over at his attorney, looking maybe a little peeved at being introduced, but Terry couldn't really tell.

"Yes, I did, or, do," he started. "Mister and missus Jeter,' he nodded at them and rubbed his hands together. "I don't want you to leave the house." He kept nodding.

"What?" Phil said, his mouth in a frown. Martin gave a smirk.

"That's good news, isn't it, Phil?" Charlene asked, looking around and obviously just as confused as Terry felt.

But it was Martin who answered. "Seems Robert here just removed one of the provisions needed for adverse possession."

"Did you do this, Martin?" Phil's face was flushed.

"No, Mr. Younger did this all on his own."

Terry tried to understand what was happening. "I don't get it." He held his hands before him, palms up.

"Well, Terry," Phil looked like he was ready to pop. "One of the things that must be in place if someone is going to get ownership through adverse possession is it must be hostile. Mr. Younger just said you can stay; therefore, it's no longer hostile."

Now Robert looked confused. He shook his head as if trying to get a gnat away from his eyes. "Martin, did you draw those papers I asked you for?" Robert waved towards the open briefcase.

"Yes, yes, I did." Martin reached into the case and brought out a folder. He handed it towards Terry, but Phil reached over and snatched it from him. Phil opened it and read while Terry stood there and started sweating again. Phil looked up at Martin and read some more. Then he looked at Robert and read some more.

"Well, what is it?" Charlene finally said a bit too loudly.

"Martin, if I could just have a word with my clients?" Phil raised his eyebrows.

"Oh, for Christ's sake, Phil, it's not a plea deal. It's an offer and a very generous one at that." Martin barked, and Phil scowled at the reprimand.

Now Robert tired of the lawyers playing catch-a-bunny.

"Terry, Charlene, I'm willing to let you all rent the place."

"Rent to own, the document says," Phil interjected, as if he were making a point in a courtroom. Terry realized then that Phil was intimidated by Martin Douglas and was trying to show off.

Terry reached over and grabbed the papers from Phil and started reading. Charlene came next to him and looked over his arm at the document. "What's it say, Honey?"

Terry looked up at Charlene, then at Robert, then back at Charlene. "He's gonna sell it to us, rent-to-own, Charlene, and the price is," he looked back at the paper to be sure he had read it right. "Well, the price is very fair." He pointed to the piece of paper at the price, then moved down to the amount of rent. Charlene was leaning into him, following his movement. It was certainly within their budget. Terry looked up at Robert again. He stood there grinning. "I don't get it," Terry finally said. "You told us we had to leave."

"Yeah, well," Robert hooked his thumbs in his pockets and looked at the ground. "I have a lot of memories in that house, family memories, mainly. Kind of figured a new family might add some memories of their own."

"You don't say," Terry looked at the man in disbelief.

"And, I just bought a little place on Hickory Creek I want to build on, so there's that." Robert glanced to his side and Susan stood next to him, the knees of her pants brown with mud. "And," Robert put his arm around his sister, "I've been told I need an income." He smiled again looking at his sister. "And maybe, if you have any extra zucchini, you might share one with me." Robert looked as happy as a lizard in the sun.

Charlene's eyes brimmed with tears looking at Robert. "I could just hug you," she finally managed.

"Hell, I could too," Terry added.

Robert chuckled and shook his head. He held his free hand up. "That's okay." And the four of them laughed and smiled for a good fifteen seconds. The two lawyers stood there, taking it all in.

"Um," Charlene finally broke the spell. "We can pay a little down payment." She looked over at Terry, a bit late, he thought. But she was right. They could pay some up front, if Uncle Robert needed some money now. Terry simply nodded.

"No, not necessary. What you all need is another car." Robert said flatly. "If I hadn't happened by . . ." He nodded towards the garden and Terry followed his line of sight to where Rose and Luke were carrying a pail of water together to water the new plants. Charlene looked back to their children and then at Terry.

Now Phil, who seemed to have disappeared while the chatter was going on, finally spoke again. "We're selling Raylene's car," he said quickly. Everyone looked at him blankly. "My cousin?" he said as if everyone in town would know who Raylene was.

"Raylene can't drive," Martin offered, and Phil looked like his eyes were going to explode.

"Only for a hundred twenty days," Phil's voice rose.

Martin looked at him evenly. "I only meant she is a poor driver, Phil." Now Phil began to quiver and breathe shallowly. "I'd have it checked out before you buy it, Mr. and Mrs. Jeter." Martin gave a friendly nod towards the two of them.

"Call me Terry," he stuck his hand out to shake with Martin.

"Charlene," she offered her hand as well.

"Well, I know a guy can look at the car," Robert said. "Can fix anything that runs or used to."

"Barlow," Martin nodded. "Best mechanic I ever saw. Good idea." Then he turned back to Phil who had wilted against the SUV. "Long as it's okay to check it out?" Phil managed a small, agreeable smile. "Well, are we ready to sign?"

Martin pulled a black and silver pen from the inside of his jacket and pulled the top off, then reached for the folder in Terry's hand.

Chapter 19

Rosie heard the screen door bang shut. She didn't turn around. That would be Lukie, since Mommy or Daddy would have called out to her to stay out of the mud or something like that. No, it was Luke. Rosie kept digging with the dented up serving spoon she had found in the kitchen drawer. The hole was just about right. Then Lukie was standing right beside her.

"What are you doing?" He asked it as if she was doing something wrong. She didn't know why he felt like he was the boss of her.

"Planting a flower." Rosie lifted her head to say, *so there.*

"Daddy won't like you digging up the garden, Rosie." He stooped down now to get a better angle.

"Daddy said this was our garden, right? We all are in this together, Daddy said, right?" She turned her head to look at her brother. He looked like his old self now. She had been so afraid that he would never be the same, but now he was okay. In fact, she had worried he might never come home from the hospital. Grandma had gone to the hospital and never come back. She was happy to see him stooping down to watch her dig, even if he was being too bossy. "Besides, there's nothing planted here."

"Yeah, well, I think he just meant we needed to weed it." He reached over and touched the small, dangling batch of roots of her flower she had dug up in the back yard. "What kind of flower you planting, Rosie?"

Rosie wanted to tell him not to touch the flower, but decided it wouldn't hurt it. But it was her flower. "It's a violet, Uncle Robert told me. He eats them." Rosie twisted her head to look at Lukie and let out a giggle. "Says they make you grow tall."

"Huh," Lukie snorted. "He musta eaten a ton of them."

Rosie gave a laugh for that one. Then she saw the worm. She pointed at the violet plant. "Look, Lukie. A worm." She dropped the spoon and picked up the small red wriggling bug and put it in her palm. She liked the way it tickled her hand when he moved around.

"Think Uncle Robert eats those too?" Lukie stood, casting a shadow across the hole Rosie had dug.

"Eww, I don't think so. But he says they're good for the plants. I'm going to put him here with my flower." Rosie picked up the worm and dropped it into the hole. She crumpled up some dirt and dropped it in the hole, then put the violet in. She put more dirt around the sides of the flower then stood to admire her work, wiping the dirt from her hands on her jumper. She turned and looked at her brother who shook his head slightly, but she didn't know what that might be about. They stood there, looking at each other, for a few moments.

"Want to play town with the cars on the porch, Rosie?" He motioned with his thumb.

"Yeah," she grinned. She loved playing with his toy cars. Lukie was a great big brother. She took off towards the house at a gallop.

About the Author

Lawrence has six books in print, four novels, one memoir, and one nonfiction. He has a contract for three more. He writes literary novels, short fiction, non-fiction articles and books, creative non-fiction, and poetry.

His work has appeared in a wide range of local, regional, and national journals. He also is a visual artist working in graphite, oils, metal and wood. Dr. Weill lives in the woods in Kentucky overlooking a beaver pond next to a wildlife preserve. He is also an avid outdoorsman and gardener.